'You are so beau

His arms held her close, [illegible] the instant stiffening of her muscles.

She wrenched out of his arms, her face flushed, her eyes tormented, as she stumbled back from him.

'I'm sorry,' she choked out, 'but I can't do this. No, don't touch me again!' she threw at him when he took a step towards her.

'You're crazy, do you know that?'

'Yes,' she replied with a funny little laugh. 'Yes. I think I must be.'

'You can't just leave without explaining yourself.'

The emotional distress in her eyes was instantly replaced with a defiant fury. 'I don't have to explain myself to you,' she spat. 'I'm going now. Don't try to stop me.'

Jason had never felt so helpless before. Or more frustrated. Logic told him to just let her go.

But then he remembered how she'd felt in his arms and he knew that he could not follow his own advice.

This wasn't over yet. Not by a long shot.

RUTHLESS

Men who can't be tamed… Or so they think!

If you love strong, commanding men—
you'll love this brand-new mini-series.

Meet the guy who breaks the rules to get exactly what he wants, because he is…

HARD-EDGED & HANDSOME
He's the man who's impossible to resist…

RICH & RAKISH
He's got everything—and needs nobody…
Until he meets one woman…

He's RUTHLESS!
In his pursuit of passion; in his
world the winner takes all!

Brought to you by your favourite
Modern Romance™ authors!

THE BILLIONAIRE BOSS'S FORBIDDEN MISTRESS

BY
MIRANDA LEE

First published in Great Britain 2006
Harlequin Mills & Boon Limited,
Eton House, 18-24 Paradise Road, Richmond, Surrey TW9 1SR

ISBN 0 263 84800 0

Set in Times Roman 10½ on 12¾ pt.
01-0406-39813

Printed and bound in Spain
by Litografia Rosés, S.A., Barcelona

CHAPTER ONE

LEAH DIDN'T STOP swimming till a full twenty laps were behind her.

Satisfied with her workout, she stroked over to the side of the pool and grabbed the silver handles on the ladder. As she hauled herself upwards out of the water, her gaze connected with her left thigh and the rough ridges of white skin that criss-crossed it.

Leah didn't look away, as she usually did. Instead, she forced herself to study the scars in the early morning sunshine.

They had faded quite a bit over the past two years. But they were never going to go away, she accepted as she climbed out on to the tiled pool surround and reached for her towel.

Leah sighed. She wished her disfigurement didn't bother her so much. It seemed pathetic to be upset about a few wretched scars when the car accident that had produced them had taken the life of her mother.

Nothing compared with that tragedy, not even Carl

leaving her a few months after the accident. Though she'd been shattered at the time.

Leah clutched the towel tightly in her hands, rubbing at her scars less than gently as she recalled the expression on Carl's face when he'd taken his first good look at her scarred leg. He'd been utterly revolted. And repulsed.

He'd made excuses not to make love to her for weeks after she came home from hospital, till finally he'd announced that he wanted a divorce, saying it was because she had changed.

Leah agreed that she had. During the long, painful weeks she'd been in hospital, she'd found a different person inside herself. A better person, she liked to think. A person with more character, and insight, and compassion.

Carl claimed she'd become far too serious and was no fun any more. Leah's desperate argument that she'd just lost her mother and was naturally feeling sad made no impression on him at all.

His leaving her had nothing to do with her personality having changed, she thought bitterly. It was all to do with her scars. And her limp.

Well, the limp had long gone but the scars would never go. Not the scars on her legs. Or the scars on her heart.

Still, she'd finally come to terms with Carl's calling it quits on her. After all, what woman would actually want to stay married to a man who could not tolerate a wife who was no longer physically perfect?

Which, before the accident, she had been. Or so she'd been told all her life.

Leah had been the image of her mother, a natural blonde with lovely green eyes, perfect teeth and skin, and a very pretty face and figure. Leah had grown up taking her good genes for granted. Taking her privileged lifestyle for granted as well.

As the only child of one of Sydney's most successful stockbrokers, she'd never wanted for a thing. She'd been spoiled rotten all her life, her pampered upbringing producing a precious little society princess who thought the world was her oyster. Working for a living had never been on Leah Bloom's agenda. She had a monthly allowance, plus a credit card. Why work nine to five in some dreary job?

When people had asked what she did for a living, she had told them she was an aspiring writer, a minor ambition that had come to her during her last year at school when her English teacher complimented her on one of her creative writing assignments. She'd even attended a fiction-writing course at one stage, bought herself a computer and started a chick-lit novel, which was little more than a diary of what she did every week.

Which meant extremely silly and shallow, Leah decided in hindsight.

How could it be anything else when her life *was* silly and shallow, every day filled with shopping and charity luncheons and idle hours spent in beauty salons getting ready for the evening's outing. By the time

Leah was twenty-one, she'd been to more parties and premieres and black-tie dos than she could count.

Falling in love and marrying Carl had been the icing on her seemingly never-ending cake. He'd been attractive and charming and rich. *Very* rich. Leah's family didn't mix with any other kind.

Carl had been thirty when they married, the heir to an absolute fortune made in diamonds. She'd been twenty-three.

They'd only been married for six months when the accident happened. Way too short a time for Carl to fall out of love with her. Leah had long come to the conclusion that she'd just been a trophy wife, a decoration on his arm to show off, a possession that he'd only valued when she'd been glitteringly perfect.

Once she'd become flawed, he hadn't wanted her any more.

'Mrs B. said to tell you breakfast will be ready in ten minutes,' a male voice called out.

Leah glanced up to see her father leaning over the balcony that adjoined the master bedroom.

Dressed in his favourite navy silk dressing-gown and with a tan that a summer of swimming and yachting had produced, her father looked much younger than his sixty-two years. Of course, he did keep himself very fit in his home gym. A thick headful of expertly dyed brown hair didn't hurt, either.

'That's the only reason I come home every weekend, you know,' she replied. 'For Mrs B.'s cooking.'

This was a lie, of course. She came home every

weekend to spend time with her father, to feel his parental affection, up close and personal.

But Leah didn't want to live at home twenty-four seven. Joachim Bloom was far too dominating a personality for that. Leah knew she would find herself giving in to him if she was always around, like her mother had. As happy as her parents had been in their marriage, Leah had always been well aware who was the boss in their relationship.

'Rubbish!' her father retorted. 'You're skinny as a rake.'

'You can never be too thin,' she quipped.

'Or too rich,' he finished for her. 'Which reminds me, daughter, there's something important I have to discuss with you over breakfast, so shake a leg.'

'The good one?' Leah shot back at him. 'Or the gimpy one?'

Pretending to her father not to care about her scars had become a habit. She didn't want him to know that they bothered her as much as they still did. Or that they were the reason she never went to the beach any more, or swam anywhere else but here, at home, when there was no one around but her father and Mrs B. to see them.

'Very funny,' he said with a roll of his eyes, and disappeared back inside.

Leah threw the towel over her shoulder and headed for her bedroom, one of six in the two-storeyed, waterside mansion that she'd been brought up in and which was probably worth many millions on the current market.

Vaucluse was *the* place to live in Sydney's eastern suburbs.

For a while after his mother's death, her father had thought of selling the house and buying elsewhere, but Leah had talked him out of it. And she was so glad she had. It was a comfort at times, to be around her mother's things. To feel her presence in the rooms.

Such beautiful rooms. Such a beautiful house, Leah thought wistfully as she climbed the curving staircase that led up to the bedrooms.

The thought didn't come to Leah till she was in the shower that her father might have changed his mind about the house. He might still want to sell. Maybe that was what he wanted to discuss with her.

I won't let him, she resolved as she snapped off the water. I'll fight him to the death!

A couple of minutes later, she was running downstairs, dressed in cut-off blue jeans and a pink singlet top, her long damp hair up in a ponytail.

Joachim's heart lurched as his daughter raced into the morning room. How like her mother she was! It was like looking at Isabel in her twenties.

'If you think you're going to sell this house, Daddy,' Leah tossed at him with a feisty look as she sat down at the breakfast table, 'then you can think again.'

Joachim sighed. Like her mother in looks, but not in personality. Isabel had been a soft sweet woman, always deferring to him. Never making waves.

Leah *looked* soft and sweet. When she'd been younger, she'd even *been* soft and sweet. But over the past eighteen months, she'd become much more assertive, and very independent. Not hard, exactly. But quite formidable and forthright.

But who could blame her for turning tough, came a more sympathetic train of thought. Carl had a lot to answer for. Fancy leaving Leah when she needed him the most. The man was a weasel and a coward. Joachim wouldn't spit on him if he was on fire.

His daughter had had two alternatives during that awful time in her life. Go to pieces, or develop a thicker skin.

For a while it had been touch and go. Joachim was very proud that Leah had eventually pulled herself together and moved on.

'No, Leah,' he told her with a reassuring smile. 'I'm not selling the house. I know how much you love it.'

Leah's relief was only temporary. Then what *did* Daddy want to talk to her about?

'What's up, then?' she asked as she reached for a slice of toast from the silver toast rack. 'You're not going to make a fuss about my working, are you? I thought you were proud of my getting a job.'

Perhaps *surprised* would have been a better description of her father's reaction. When Leah had first mentioned a year ago that she was going to find a job, her stunned father had asked her what on earth she thought she could do.

'Even waitresses have to have experience these days!' he'd told her.

Leah understood his scepticism after she went to have her resumé done. Because there was nothing much she could put on it, except a very average pass in her Higher School certificate—studying had not been high on Leah's society princess agenda—plus that very brief creative writing course. She had absolutely no qualifications for employment other than her social skills and her looks and a limited ability to use a computer.

Which was why the only job she'd been able to find after attending endless interviews was as a receptionist. Not at some flashy establishment in the city, either. She currently worked for a company that manufactured beauty products, and had their factory and head office at Ermington, a mainly industrial suburb in western Sydney.

'I *am* proud of your getting that job,' her father insisted. 'Extremely.'

Mrs B., coming in with a plate piled high with scrambled eggs, hash browns, fried tomato and bacon, interrupted their conversation for a moment.

'This looks delicious, Mrs B.,' Leah complimented her father's housekeeper as she placed the plate in front of her.

Leah was privately thankful that she only had to eat Mrs B.'s breakfast one day a week, or she'd have a backside as big as a bus.

'Just make sure you eat it all,' Mrs B. said with a

sharp glance at Leah. 'You're getting way too thin, missie.'

'You won't catch yourself another husband with that waif look, you know,' her father agreed.

Leah could have pointed out that she turned down several offers of dates every week. Instead, she smiled sweetly and tucked into the food till Mrs B. left the room. Then she put down her knife and fork and looked straight at her father.

'I have no intention of getting married again, Daddy.'

'What? Why not?'

'You know why not.'

'Not every man is as weak as Carl,' he grumbled. 'You're a beautiful young woman, Leah. You should have a husband. And babies.'

'I don't want to argue about this, Daddy. I just want you to know my feelings on the matter so that I don't have to put up with that kind of comment any more.'

'You'll change your mind,' he said. 'One day, you'll meet the right man and fall in love and that will be that. Nature will have her way with you. You mark my words.'

Leah suppressed a sigh. She'd been marking her father's words all her life. She loved him to death, but over the past two years she'd come to realise he was an incredible bossy-boots who thought he knew what was best for everyone.

'Can we move on, please?' she said, picking up a piece of crispy bacon with her fingers, and munching into it. 'You wanted to discuss something with me?' she asked between swallows. 'I presume it didn't have anything to do with my remarrying. It sounded like it was about money. Which reminds me. Don't start telling me what I can and cannot do with the income from my trust fund, either. It is my money to do with as I please. Mum made no conditions on her legacy in her will. If I want to give it all away, I can. Not that I am. *Yet.* At the moment, I have to keep some back each month to make ends meet.'

'I don't wonder,' her father said. 'From what I recall, you only earn a pittance.'

'The women in the factory earn even less,' Leah pointed out. 'Yet some of them bring up a family on their salary. My aim is to support myself on my salary alone. It will do my character good to see how the other half lives. It's just taking a while for my champagne taste to catch up with my beer income. Now, what did you want to talk to me about?' she asked, and munched into the bacon again.

'Eat your breakfast first. I see you're enjoying it. We'll talk over coffee afterwards.'

Leah's curiosity was intense by the time she cleared her plate and picked up her coffee cup. 'Well?' she said after a couple of sips. 'Out with it.'

'What do you know about the takeover of Beville Holdings?'

'What? You mean it's a done deal?' Leah asked with alarm in her voice. So far there had only been rumours at work of a possible takeover. But lots of Leah's fellow employees were genuinely worried.

Leah had heard from more than one source that when companies were taken over, they were invariably subjected to 'restructuring'. Leah had been chatting to one of their newest reps on Friday, a really nice man with a wife and young family. He told Leah that new management always pruned staff and usually adopted a policy of last-in-first-out, regardless of ability. Apparently, Peter had lost his previous job that way and was worried sick about the same thing happening again.

'Yes, it's a done deal,' her father confirmed. 'There's an article about it in the business section of the Sunday paper here. Plus a photo of your new boss, Jason Pollack.'

'Jason Pollack,' Leah repeated, the name not ringing a bell. 'Never heard of him.' Leah might not have joined the work force till late in her life, but she'd been brought up on dinner table discussions about the wheeler dealers of this world whose faces and names often graced the dailies.

'Not all that many people have,' her father informed her. 'He keeps a very low media profile.'

'Show me,' she said, and her father passed across the relevant pages.

'Goodness!' Leah exclaimed, having expected to see a photo of a man who was at least middle aged. And a good deal fatter.

Takeover tycoons were rarely this young. Or this slim.

Or this handsome.

Something inside Leah tightened when her eyes met those of Jason Pollack's. Dark brown, they were. And deeply set, hooded by eyebrows that were as straight and uncompromising as his mouth. His hair was black. And wavy. Brushed neatly back from his high forehead with no part. His nose was straight, with widely flared nostrils, his jawline squared off, with a small dimple in its centre.

'Is this an old photo?' she asked brusquely.

'Nope,' her father said. 'If you read the article, you'll see he's only thirty-six. He's very good looking, isn't he?'

'I suppose so,' Leah said. 'If you like the type.' Which she obviously did. She couldn't take her eyes off him.

Yet he was nothing like Carl, who'd been big and blond, a Nordic giant of a man with a raw-boned handsomeness.

Jason Pollack's face had a model-like quality, probably because of the perfect symmetry of his finely sculptured features.

Yet no one would mistake him for a male model. There was an air about him that was unmistakably magnate material. A maturity in his eyes—and an intelligence—that Leah found both attractive and irritating.

Irritating because she didn't want to find the new boss of Beville Holdings in any way attractive. She didn't want to find *any* man attractive for a long, long time.

'How on earth did he get to be so rich and successful so young?' she queried sharply. 'I know he's not old money. I would have met him before, if he was.'

'Nope. He was an immigrant from Poland, brought over here by his father after his mother died in childbirth. He grew up in the Western suburbs and never even went to university. Started in sales straight out of school.'

'Must have been a *very* good salesman to acquire so much in such a short time,' Leah said.

'Seems so. But he also married into money when he was in his late twenties. His wife was his first employer's widow. Her husband owned the WhizzBiz Electronics chain of shops. Jason Pollack sold himself to his new lady boss within a year of her husband's demise. She herself died of cancer a couple of years later, leaving her adored young husband everything. Admittedly, by then, he had reversed WhizzBiz's dwindling sales. After his wife's death, he sold the whole chain for an enormous price. That's become Pollack's trademark. He buys ailing companies, fixes them up, then sells them.

'But only if he thinks fixing is feasible,' her father continued whilst Leah kept staring at Jason Pollack's photo. 'He reveals in that article that on one occasion, after he gained access to the company's records and employees, he judged that a salvage operation simply wasn't on. So he cut his losses and dismantled the company altogether, selling off whatever assets were involved.'

'Regardless of the poor employees,' she scorned.

'I gather he gave each of them more than their entitlements.'

'Which he could well afford,' she snapped, dragging her eyes away from Jason Pollack to scan the rest of the article. The man had to be worth squillions, his current residence being the top floor of a skyscraper in the middle of Sydney's city and business district.

'Maybe, but he didn't have to, Leah. The man has a good reputation for being more than fair. Look, Beville Holdings has not made a profit for two years now. That's what I wanted to talk to you about. Whether Beville Holdings is salvageable, or not?'

Leah frowned. 'Why do you want to know?'

'I happen to own a nice little parcel of Beville Holdings shares. Bought them two years ago when they were rock bottom. Are they going to increase in value?'

'According to this article they've already gone up a lot.'

'Yes, but they'll go up a lot more in the end if Pollack can work his usual miracle. So tell me, daughter, can your company be turned around, or do you think your new boss will sell it off in pieces?'

'How on earth would *I* know?' Leah replied, tossing the paper back over to her father to stop herself from staring at the infernal man any more.

'Come now, Leah, don't be coy. You're one of those girls everyone tells everything to. People like to confide in you. I've seen it for myself many times. You've been at that company for over eight months now. I'll bet you know exactly what's going on there. Just because you didn't put your mind to your studies at school doesn't mean you didn't inherit my brains. You're smart as a whip, when you want to be.'

'I wasn't too smart when I married Carl.'

'That's different. Love can make a fool of even the smartest person. Now give me an honest opinion. Is my investment going to grow?'

Leah thought about all the information she had gleaned at work over the past few months.

Her father was right. People did like to confide in her. More so now than ever. Since the accident, she'd developed a genuinely compassionate ear, whereas before, her being a good listener had just been a social skill, learned from her mother.

Leah knew exactly what was wrong with Beville Holdings. The problems were fixable. *If* the new boss knew where to look, and whose advice to take.

'Beville Holdings has excellent products,' came her carefully worded reply. 'But poor management. I think your shares will increase in value.'

Joachim smiled. Smart girl, his daughter. Smart and beautiful and not cut out to spend her life being a receptionist out in the boondocks. Or for living alone, for that matter.

Joachim could understand that her husband's defection had hurt her terribly. But life went on.

Leah was only twenty-six. Time for her to start dating again. But he couldn't force the issue. He'd have to be subtle. Maybe he'd surprise her with a dinner party for next Saturday night, invite a few old friends, people he knew she liked. But he'd also slip in someone new, some handsome, highly eligible young man who might impress her.

But who?

Joachim couldn't think of anyone. With a sigh he picked up the paper again and found himself staring down at the photograph of Jason Pollack. Suddenly, a voice whispered to him that he should invite *him*. Jason Pollack.

Joachim's first reaction was hell, no. Not some ambitious bastard who'd married for money. But the voice insisted. If he hadn't known better, he would have thought it was Isabel, whispering to him. Isabel, who hadn't liked Carl one bit and who'd said Leah needed to marry a different type of man. A stronger, self-made man.

Isabel had been right about Carl.

Jason Pollack was a strong man, Joachim told himself. And a self-made man. A man who could probably do with a new wife. A younger one this time who could give him children.

Joachim still had his doubts, but that soft voice was very persistent.

All right, he whispered back in his head.

Don't tell Leah, the voice added.

Joachim flicked a quick glance across the table at his daughter.

'What?' she said.

'Nothing. Nothing.'

But the die was set. He would invite Pollack to dinner, and he would not tell Leah. Which left him with the problem of getting her to attend. Not an easy task.

But he would persuade her. Somehow.

CHAPTER TWO

LEAH TURNED INTO the driveway of Beville Holdings, stopping at the security gate and smiling over at Ted, the man who manned the gate on the morning shift. Usually, he just smiled back and pressed the button that lifted the barrier, allowing her to drive through.

Today, Ted slid back the window and waved for Leah to wind her window down. Which she did.

'He's here,' he called to her in a conspiratorial voice. 'The new boss.'

'What?' Leah's stomach twisted into an instant knot. She'd expected Jason Pollock to show up at work sooner or later, but not this soon.

'Didn't you read about the takeover in yesterday's paper?' Ted asked her.

'Er...no, I didn't,' Leah replied, not wanting to seem too on the ball. She didn't exactly play a blonde bimbo role at work, but at the same time, she didn't drop any clues over who she really was. She liked it that she was treated as a simple working-class girl from Gladesville.

No one at Beville Holdings had ever been to her waterview apartment or connected her surname—Johannsen—with the diamond dynasty.

'Well, his name is Mr Pollack and he arrived over an hour ago to check out the factory. He'll be heading over to your section soon, I'll bet, so just as well you're not late.'

'What's he like?' Leah asked, her curiosity getting the better of her.

'Not too bad. I think my job's safe. When he drove up to the gate just after seven and announced who he was, I still asked him for ID, and he seemed to like that.'

'Good for you. What's he driving? A flash car, I'll bet.'

'A dark blue sporty one.'

Leah's top lip curled. Typical. Her father had declared yesterday that Jason Pollack *wasn't* some kind of playboy—despite his living in a penthouse.

But men like that always ran true to form. Give a man money and he didn't choose to putter around in anything small, or sedate. Rich people picked cars that supposedly reflected their personality, and power.

Leah had once zipped around Sydney in a red, top-of-the-range roadster, a present from her father on her twenty-first birthday. She'd traded it in for a white, second-hand hatchback when she got this job, not wanting anyone at work to think of her as a rich bitch. She wanted to be liked for herself, not her money.

'Thanks for the warning, Ted,' Leah said, and drove

on, turning into the staff car park, which was surprisingly full. All the managers' cars were there, an unusual occurrence for this hour on a Monday morning. They must have heard about the takeover, too, and decided to put their best feet forward.

The only empty car space in the row nearest the main office building was right next to a dark blue sports car.

Leah hesitated, then slid her vehicle in next to it, determined not to surrender to these silly nerves, which were currently turning her insides into a washing machine.

He was just a man, for pity's sake. She'd met men just as attractive. And just as rich. Heck, she'd been married to one!

Okay, so she'd found Jason Pollack's photo extremely attractive. So what?

Once she actually met the man, his undoubtedly up-himself personality would soon stop these ridiculous stomach flutters.

Admittedly, a dark blue sports car suggested that Jason Pollack wasn't a total show pony, like her ex. Carl would have rocked up in something flashy and gold, or silver. That was exactly what she'd seen Carl sitting in the last time their paths crossed. Something flashy and silver.

Leah climbed out from behind the wheel and walked round to her passenger side, opening the door there to retrieve her handbag and peeping into the blue sports car at the same time.

Not a thing on the leather seats, or on the floor. Nothing to give her a glimpse of Jason Pollack's character. Except that it looked like he was neat freak. There wasn't a single piece of rubbish anywhere. Or a spot of dirt. The car gleamed in the morning sun, both inside and outside.

People like that were usually very critical, and controlling.

'Better get a move on then, girlie,' she muttered to herself as she zapped the lock on her key and hurried up the path that led to the head office, a rectangular brick building built in the early sixties, but which had been totally renovated late last year.

You couldn't tell by looking at the place that Beville Holdings hadn't made a profit lately. You'd think everything was coming up roses.

Pushing through the front door, Leah headed across the deserted reception area straight for the nearby powder room. Her wrist watch said twenty-three minutes past eight. She only had five minutes to check her appearance before she was due to be sitting behind the semi-circular reception desk, looking cool, calm and collected.

Despite her self-lecturing, Leah felt anything but.

Jason said goodbye to the factory foreman, thanking him for his help, but brushing aside the man's offer to accompany him over to the head office.

Jason wanted to think. And he thought better when he was by himself.

He walked slowly along the well-signed path, wondering what he was doing, buying a company that made shower gels, shampoos, sunscreens and moisturisers. What in hell did he know about such products?

Nothing at all.

Still, he supposed retail was retail. Get the advertising right and good sales usually followed.

Judging by their performance over the last two years, Beville Holdings had not got their advertising right. Either that, or they were charging too much for their products. Or their management was less than efficient.

Jason wished he'd done some more market research before plunging in last Friday and buying a controlling share.

Never in his life before had he bought a company because of a dream. A *dream*, for pity's sake!

It had happened last Saturday night, the night he'd broken up with Hilary. He'd been upset because she'd been upset, and the last thing he'd ever wanted to do was to hurt Hilary.

They'd met just over six months ago, at a dinner party that Jason had been persuaded to attend, and which had been cripplingly boring till Hilary winked at him from across the table. Later, he'd discovered that their hostess had been doing some match-making, Hilary having not long been divorced. She was his age, slim, dark, and very attractive, as well as intelligent and confident. Jason had ended up in bed with her that night, his first woman since Karen's death four years earlier. His libido had finally bypassed his grief and come to life again, and, having come to life, wasn't going to stay silent any more.

In hindsight, Jason was amazed that he'd stayed celibate for so long. Sex had always been very important to him.

He'd first discovered the pleasures of the flesh when he'd been sixteen, his partner an older girl of nineteen who knew a thing or two. She'd lived two doors down from him, and she'd spent many a Saturday afternoon during one long hot summer, showing Jason exactly how to please her, and vice versa. When her family moved, Jason had been devastated for a while. At sixteen, it had been impossible to separate lust and love.

Eventually, he'd recovered from his broken heart, and, after that, never been without a girlfriend. Though he'd never fallen in love again.

Till he met Karen.

Jason smiled softly to himself as he thought of his wife.

Another older woman, but this time fifteen years older. Forty-two to his twenty-seven. Yet they'd been perfect together. And so ecstatically happy.

Of course, everyone else thought he'd married his boss's widow out of cold-blooded ambition. Hilary probably hadn't believed him when he had said he'd loved his wife.

Jason supposed it was only reasonable that, after sleeping with Hilary every weekend for six months, she might expect him to propose.

In his defence, he'd made it clear right from the start of their relationship that he wasn't interest in remarrying.

But last Saturday night, Hilary had started pressing for him to marry her and he knew he couldn't. Because, as attractive as Hilary was, he just wasn't in love with her, and once you'd been in love—really, deeply in love—you couldn't settle for less.

After Hilary flounced out, saying she never wanted to see him again, he hadn't been able to sleep. So he'd popped one of the sleeping pills that the doctor had prescribed for him after Karen died and which were hopelessly out of date. But at the time, he hadn't cared. He just wanted oblivion.

But his sleep had been full of dreams, mostly of Karen, telling him—as she often had during that final awful week—that he wasn't to grieve, that, one day, he'd meet someone else, someone more right for him than she'd been, someone who'd give him babies and a wonderful life.

Silly dreams, because Jason knew that wouldn't happen.

And then, seemingly only seconds before he woke, had come this other odd, startlingly vivid dream.

He was driving out in the country and suddenly, in the middle of a mown paddock, he saw this massive bill-board with a blonde on it. She'd been photographed from the back from her hips up, and was naked. The effect was incredibly sexual. She had a slender but curvy shape, porcelain-like skin and dead straight, glisteningly golden hair streaming halfway down her bare back. Her arms were stretched up in front of her, tossing a bottle of shampoo up into a bright blue sky, golden rays coming out from it as if it were the sun. Across the bottom of the billboard were the words: START EVERY DAY WITH SUNSHINE.

Jason had driven right off the road in the dream as he stared at the blonde, the accident jolting him awake. He'd been relieved to find it was only a dream, but the image on that bill-board had stayed in his mind all day, tantalising him. Haunting him.

He knew he'd never seen such an ad before. He *had* heard of a brand name called Sunshine. Vaguely. But he thought it was attached to cleaning stuff, not shampoo.

That evening, he'd rung Harry Wilde—Harry ran an advertising agency he used occasionally—and asked him if he knew of Sunshine shampoo, or of such an ad.

He hadn't.

Jason had then gone to an all-hours supermarket and found that there was indeed a range of products with the Sunshine label, all made by a company called Beville Holdings. Further investigation via his broker revealed Beville Holdings was a small but well-established manufacturing company, owned by a parent company in England. Their shares were quite low, due to their not making a profit and not declaring a decent dividend for the past two years.

'And a week later, here I am,' Jason muttered to himself. 'The owner of said profitless company.'

Jason found himself standing outside the main door of the head office building, shaking his head wryly up the Beville Holdings sign. He didn't really believe in fate, or karma. In the main, he was a practical man.

But he could not deny that he'd been less than practical this past week. That crazy dream had robbed him of his savvy approach to business. As soon as he'd found out there was a real company that made Sunshine products, he'd felt compelled to buy the place, without doing any solid market research, a process that normally took many weeks.

Bob had thought he'd lost his marbles.

Still, if he listened to Bob all the time, he'd never buy anything. Bob was a great PA, but not the most decisive of men. Not a risk taker in any way, shape or form.

Businessmen had to take risks, occasionally. In the main, however, they were informed risks. Jason had to admit that, this time, he'd gone out on a limb.

Still, it could be an interesting project, he told himself, turning Beville Holdings around. A real challenge. He'd been getting into a rut lately.

Success would depend on what he discovered in here, Jason decided as he pushed through the half-glass door. If serious problems lay in the sales and marketing departments, things could get tricky.

Golden handshakes were the only answer for getting rid of bad management, and that was very costly.

So was this décor, Jason realised as he set foot on the plush jade carpet that covered the spacious reception area. His eyebrows lifted as he glanced at the cream leather seating and the expensively framed watercolours that graced the cream walls, his thoughtful gaze finally resting on the very modern, but very unmanned reception desk.

He was glancing at the time on his watch—it was eight twenty-seven—when a movement caught the corner of his eye. Jason turned in time to see a young woman emerge from the ladies' room across the way.

Jason's heart skipped a beat.

She was blonde, and beautiful, wearing a pale green dress that clung to her perfect breasts and swished around her perfect legs. She seemed startled when she saw him, stopping in mid-stride. But then, with a toss of her lovely head, she headed in his direction, her hips swaying provocatively.

'Good morning, Mr Pollack,' she said crisply as she stretched out her hand towards him. 'I'm sorry I wasn't here to greet you when you came in, but I'm not due to start till eight thirty.'

So she knew who he was, did she? Probably saw his photo in the paper yesterday, Jason realised as he took her hand, holding it within both of his as he absorbed more of her incredible beauty at closer quarters.

'That's perfectly all right, Miss…er…'

'Johannsen,' she supplied. 'Leah Johannsen. I…I'm the receptionist here at Beville Holdings.'

Jason knew lots of companies hired lookers to man their front desk, but this girl was totally wasted here. She could have been a model, she was so striking.

Those eyes. That mouth. That stunning hair. So shiny and silky looking, with just the hint of a wave as it rippled down over her slender shoulders.

It made you want to touch it. Kiss it. Wrap it around your…

Jason gave himself a severe mental shake, hoping his face did not reflect his thoughts. Indulging in that type of sexual fantasy was not Jason's usual bent.

But once the image filled his mind, it was joined by others. To his annoyance, his flesh soon followed and he found himself glancing down at her left hand to see if she was wearing any rings.

The shot of adrenalin that came when he saw that her fingers were bare startled Jason. It wasn't like him to lose it over a pretty girl.

But of course this girl wasn't just pretty. She was perfection.

And suddenly, he wanted her. Wanted her more than he'd ever wanted Hilary.

But then he hadn't ever really wanted Hilary as such, had he? He'd just wanted regular sex. Any attractive woman would have done.

But you really want *this* girl, came a voice from inside that Jason didn't recognise. It was dark and driven and utterly ruthless. You want her and you're going to have her, come hell or high water!

CHAPTER THREE

IT FELT LIKE an eternity to Leah before Jason Pollack let her hand go.

But maybe that was just her imagination. Time seemed to have slowed down since she came out of the ladies' room and found her new boss standing just inside the main door, looking over at her.

His photo hadn't done him justice. But then, how could a two-dimensional head-and-shoulders shot capture the essence of such a man?

Yesterday, Leah had thought his dark, deeply set eyes had exuded magnate material. In the flesh, they exuded something else, a powerful magnetism that had pulled at her from across the room.

She'd been unable to breathe for a moment. Unable to move. But then her pride—and a measure of pique—had come to her rescue, snapping her out of her fatuous state and propelling her towards him with cool eyes and creditable composure. She even managed to observe—and ruefully admire—his taste in clothes.

His black, single-breasted business suit was sleek and expensive, tailored to compliment his tall, elegantly lean body. He'd matched it with a deep blue shirt that highlighted his olive skin. His silvery grey tie was classy, and nicely understated. So was his watch, also silver, with a black leather band.

By the time she reached him, Leah imagined—mistakenly, as it turned out—that she could shake his hand and come away unscathed.

But the moment his hands—*both* of them—enclosed hers, she'd been totally rattled, reduced to stammering when he asked her name.

Yet she never stammered. Or felt swamped by the kind of feelings that had overtaken her.

Within moments, she'd wanted to forget where she was and who he was. When he'd stared deep into her eyes, she'd dissolved inside. When he'd glanced down at her left hand—rather pointedly, she'd thought—she'd wanted to blurt out that, yes, she was free, free to do whatever he wanted, wherever he wanted, whenever he wanted it.

The wanton submissiveness that overwhelmed her had been mind-blowing. And totally shocking. Leah had never experienced anything like it. Not even with Carl, whom she'd loved.

But this had nothing to do with love, Leah realised shakily after he released her hand.

His no longer touching her helped Leah gather herself a little. Now, if only he would stop looking at her the way he was looking at her, she might be able to pull herself totally together. But he continued to gobble her up with his eyes.

Leah knew men found her attractive. What was on show, that is. Jason Pollack might not be so interested if she revealed her left thigh to him.

Thinking about her scars did what it always did to Leah. Brought her sharply back to the real world, reminding her also that Jason Pollack had once married an older woman for money, a crime on a par with marrying a girl for her physical perfection alone. The last man on earth Leah would want to become involved with was another cold-blooded, conscienceless devil who had a computer chip for a heart.

Even if he was the sexiest man she'd ever met!

'I must get to my desk, Mr Pollack,' she said, her manner and tone suitably frosty. 'It's gone eight thirty.' And, turning her back on him, she walked with stiffly held shoulders to her work station, not looking back at him as she settled herself at her desk.

But she could feel his eyes still on her, burning right through her clothes.

Jim Matheson charging down the hallway into the reception area was a godsend.

'Mr Pollack! So there you are! They just rang from the factory to say you left some time ago. Leah, why didn't you let us know Mr Pollack was here?' Jim snapped at her.

'I've only just walked in,' came the new boss's smooth reply before she could defend herself. 'And, please, make it Jason. I don't stand on ceremony. And you'd be?'

'Jim. Jim Matheson. I'm the national sales manager here at Beville Holdings.'

And the biggest creep in the place, thought Leah. Matheson had made a pass at her on her very first day, but she'd soon put him in his place. Still, he hadn't forgotten and was never nice to her.

'Jim,' the new boss said warmly, coming forward to shake his hand. 'Nice to meet you. And you too, Leah,' he added, throwing her a look and a small smile that carried several subtle messages which Leah understood only too well.

One—I'm interested.

Two—You don't fool me for a minute with that cold-shoulder act.

And three—I'll get back to you later.

A shiver ran down Leah's spine as she watched the two men walk together down the corridor that led to the sales and marketing divisions. He was going to ask her out. She could feel it. He was going to ask her out and she wasn't going to have the willpower to say no.

But by lunchtime that day, events hadn't developed quite as Leah had expected. For one thing, she hadn't set eyes on Jason Pollack again that morning. He'd stayed down in Jim's office, having meetings with the various section managers. She'd been informed of this by the general office girl who relieved Leah at the reception desk at eleven every day so she could have her morning tea break.

Mandy hadn't met the great man herself, but she'd

already heard on the grapevine that he was a hunk of the first order. All good-looking men were hunks to Mandy, who was eighteen, a slightly plump, rosy-faced girl with an infectious smile and a happy manner.

Leah had spent her morning tea break in the canteen, listening to the gossip from the factory girls who were there, having their lunch break, as their hours were from seven till three. Leah got sick and tired of hearing how drop-dead gorgeous the new boss was.

Leah had returned to her desk, resenting Jason Pollack all the more because she knew he was being gushed over, mainly because for his looks. She'd learned to hate that kind of superficial attraction, yet there she was, suffering from it herself.

Trays of coffee and food had appeared from the canteen around twelve thirty, delivered to Jim's office by two of the female kitchen hands who'd been literally swooning as they hurried back past reception.

'He's so hot!' Leah heard one of them say. 'And he smiled at me.'

'He smiled at me too, honey,' the older woman said. A bit more drily. 'He's a charmer all right. But don't get your hopes up. Men like that don't take out waitresses,' she added as they both swept out the door.

Or receptionists, Leah realised with a perverse rush of disappointment.

What a fool she'd been, getting herself all het up over nothing. He hadn't been coming on to her earlier. He was just being his so-called charming self. Hadn't her father said Jason Pollack had originally been a top salesmen?

Since working here, Leah had met quite a few salesmen and most of them had the gift of the gab. Most of them were good-looking men, too. And outrageous flirts. There wasn't a sales rep at Beville Holdings who hadn't asked her out. And that included the married ones.

Except for Peter. The one with the sick wife. *He'd* never asked her out. That was why Leah liked him so much. He was a really decent guy. Honest and hard working, unlike some of the others around here. If Jason Pollack even thought about making Peter redundant, she would have something to say about it.

No, she would have *a lot* to say about it. After all, what was the worst that could happen to her? Okay, so she could lose her job. Not a total disaster, since she didn't rely on her salary to survive. Unlike poor Peter.

But she wouldn't go quietly. She'd take Prince Charming to the unfair dismissal board if he dared do that. She'd take him to the unfair dismissal board if he sacked Peter as well! She'd make him wish he'd never bought Beville Holdings before she was finished. That's what she'd do!

'Would you come and have lunch with me, Leah?'

Leah's head snapped up to find Trish standing there, looking anxious. Trish was Jim's secretary, an attractive redhead in her late twenties who deserved better, in Leah's opinion, than to be sleeping with her married boss.

Of all the women who worked at Beville Holdings, Leah liked Trish the most. They often had lunch together out on the lawns, and Leah usually sat with Trish when they all trundled down to the local pub for drinks after work every Friday night.

Trish claimed she wanted a husband and children of her own, but wouldn't listen to Leah's advice to break it off with Jim and find herself someone who was free. The last time they'd had a woman-to-woman chat over lunch, Trish had confided to Leah that Jim promised to leave his wife when his kids were older.

Famous last words!

Leah didn't really want to hear more of the same today, but Trish was Jim's secretary, with whom Jason Pollack had been installed all morning. Much as Leah despised her own ongoing curiosity and breathless interest, she jumped at the chance of finding out more about the man.

'Be right with you,' she returned. 'Just let me turn on the answering machine. I have to stop at the loo on the way as well.'

'Me, too,' Trish said.

Five minutes later, they were sitting at one of the wooden tables under the clump of willow trees behind their building, a lovely shady spot for eating outdoors on a summer's day. The humidity of January had finally gone—as had the summer storms—February so far having the kind of beautiful weather that brought tourists to Sydney in droves.

Trish had her lunch with her—sandwiches and juice brought from home. Leah hadn't quite got into that kind of budgeting as yet, and had a standard order with the canteen for a no-butter salad sandwich, low-fat muffin and black coffee, which she collected every day right on one.

'The new boss keeping you busy?' she said as soon as they sat down.

'I'll say,' Trish told her as she unwrapped her ham and tomato sandwiches. 'Under those disarming smiles of his, he's a regular power house, and very clued-up. He's had Jim answering some sticky questions, I can tell you. I think Jim's a bit worried.'

'And so he should be,' Leah said wryly.

'What do you mean?'

'You know what I mean, Trish. There's been a lot of money wasted around here. That very expensive Christmas party last year, for instance. Not to mention the sales conference at one of the most expensive resorts in Australia. Then there was the total refurbishing of the offices. To top it off, the whole sales fleet of company cars have just been replaced after only being on the road one year, with all the managers getting more expensive models.'

'When you put it like that, things could look bad.'

Leah could have also added that the new field sales manager hadn't gotten her job because of her experience in the position. The only position Shelley had experience in were those in the *Kama Sutra.*

Trish wasn't the only little dolly bird Jim had on the side. How Trish didn't know about Shelley constantly amazed her. All the reps knew. Heck, just about everyone here knew. Except Trish.

Leah didn't have the heart to tell the girl herself. She'd find out what a rat Jim was soon enough.

'A man like Jason Pollack is going to put it all together like *that* in no time flat,' Leah said, snapping her fingers.

Trish looked worried. 'Jim might get the sack.'

Now *there* was a satisfying thought. Leah believed in bastards getting their comeuppances.

The trouble was, they rarely did. From what she'd heard, Carl was as happy as Larry with a new fiancée, some stunning, up-and-coming actress who no doubt didn't have a single physical flaw.

As for Jim... He was a clever and consummate liar. He'd probably worm his way out of things. Or end up with a golden handshake, plus another top sales job somewhere else. Jim was only in his early forties, a good-looking man who could be very impressive when he wanted to be.

His silly wife *adored* him.

No, bastards didn't always get their comeuppances in life, came Leah's cynical thought. Take the new boss himself. He'd have to be a right bastard, marrying a much older woman for her money like that. And what happens? She conveniently died after no time at all, leaving him scads of money, plus the freedom to do exactly what he liked for the rest of his life.

How convenient!

'It's all very worrying,' Trish said, having not yet touched a bite of her lunch.

A wave of sympathy pushed aside Leah's sarcastic thoughts.

'*You* don't have to worry,' Leah said, reaching across to touch Trish gently on her arm. 'You haven't done anything wrong.'

'Haven't I?' Trish's eyes suddenly filled. 'I've been sleeping with a married man, Leah. Trying to take him away from his wife and family. That's not right. I know she loves him. And so do his kids. My mother would be utterly ashamed of me, if she knew…'

Leah handed over the paper napkin that came with her lunch, shaking her head as Trish made a right mess of her makeup with her tears.

'Break it off with him, Trish,' she advised. 'Give yourself a chance to find someone else.'

'It's all very well for you to say that, Leah,' Trish said with a flash of envious eyes as she mopped up her tears. 'You could get any man you want. Just look at you. You're utterly gorgeous, and you're not even wearing much makeup.'

'Skin-deep beauty is not all it's cracked up to be, Trish. Or a recipe for success with men. My first husband dumped me.'

Trish blinked her surprise. '*What?* I didn't even know you'd been married!'

Leah had carefully avoided mentioning Carl. When she'd filled in her application form she'd put single as her status. And when she chatted with the girls at work, she always carefully steered the conversations round to their lives, not hers.

When they occasionally asked her about her love life, she always said she was between boyfriends.

When any of her co-workers asked her on a Monday morning what she'd done that weekend, she say she'd gone home to visit her widowed father. She had admitted she'd lost her mother in a car accident not long back, but had never mentioned her marriage. Or her hated scars.

'How long were you married for?' Trish asked.

'Six months.'

'He left you after six months!'

Leah smiled a dry smile at Trish's bug-eyed surprise. 'Why do you think I'm a bit cynical at times?'

'I don't think you're cynical. I think you're very nice.'

Leah laughed. 'Scratch the surface and you'll find a bitter divorcée.'

'Really? Well, at least that explains why you don't have a boyfriend. I was beginning to think you were having an affair with a married man too, and didn't want to admit it. But I can see now that that's not your style.'

'Certainly not,' Leah said. 'And, Trish, please don't mention my marriage to anyone.'

'Why not? People wonder about you, you know.'

'What? *Why?*'

'Because you're clearly too good for this job, Leah. It's not just the way you look, but the way you talk, and walk. You went to one of those schools, didn't you? The kind that does deportment and stuff. I'll bet you were an aspiring model at one stage. Or an actress.'

'I...er...yes, I did do a modelling course once,' she

admitted. Her grandmother had given it to her for her sixteenth birthday.

Dear Gran. She was gone now, too. Along with her mother.

'Eat up,' Leah advised, not wanting to think about sad things any more. 'And give that Jim the flick.'

'I'll try,' Trish said, but didn't look too sure.

Leah returned to work in a depressed mood. Talking about relationships was a real downer, especially ones which had no chance of working out.

Jason Pollack remained incognito, having moved on the human resources division for the afternoon, according to Mandy when she stopped for a chat of her way to post the day's mail. By four, Leah was living in nervous anticipation of his walking by on his way out. But he didn't, even though she lingered a few minutes after her normal knock-off time of four thirty.

'I can get any man I want, can I?' she muttered irritably to herself as she finally made her way to the almost empty car park.

Only a couple of the managers' cars remained, plus the dark blue sports car.

Not that she really wanted Jason Pollack, she told herself. She'd have to be crazy to want a man like him, except perhaps on a purely physical basis. He might be all right for a wild fling. If she was the kind of girl who had wild flings. Which she wasn't.

Never had been, really. There again, sex had never been a driving need with Leah.

She'd had awful trouble with her early boyfriends, fighting them off and finding all sorts of excuses not to sleep with them. Some of them had called her frigid. Others had tolerated her saying no to their advances, perhaps because they had their eye more on her money than her body.

And then Carl had come along.

Leah had fallen madly in love for the first time and been more than happy to go to bed with Carl.

He'd been intrigued by her virginity—to begin with.

In hindsight, Leah wondered if her lack of sexual experience had been a contributing factor in his eventually leaving her. She had to confess that she wasn't the most adventurous person in bed.

As she opened her car door and just stood there, letting the heat out for a minute, Leah found herself thinking that Trish probably stayed with Jim because they had great sex together. Every single time.

She hadn't thought of that.

But was that kind of sexual pleasure and satisfaction so damned wonderful that it made you lose your head, that it made you let yourself be used, even though you knew the relationship was going nowhere?

'Are you waiting for me?'

The heat escaping from the car was nothing to the heat that filled Leah's face as she whirled to face Jason Pollack.

He looked just as good as he had that morning. Maybe even better.

'Of course not!' she denied even as her eyes drank him in. 'I was waiting till the car cooled down.'

His eyes narrowed on hers, as though he was trying to gauge the truth of her statement. 'Pity.'

What could she possibly say to that?

He closed her passenger door, which was blocking his entrance into his car, gazing at her over the rather low roof of her hatchback.

'So I'd be wasting my time if I asked you out to dinner tonight?' he said, his eyes remaining locked with her.

She stared back at him, willing herself to say no.

'Just dinner, Mr Pollack?' she managed to throw at him in a wonderfully haughty fashion.

'But of course, Ms Johanssen,' came his suave reply, those dark, sexy eyes of his telling her an entirely different story. If she agreed to dinner with him, she was definitely on the menu for afters.

'If that's all *you* want,' he added.

That did it! That tipped the scales back in favour of reason.

'What I want, Mr Pollack,' she said sharply, 'is for you to leave me alone. Please do not ask me to go out with you again, or I will report you for sexual harassment. Do I make myself clear?'

She didn't wait for him to answer. She climbed in behind the wheel, slammed the car door and gunned her engine.

Thank goodness the car park was nearly empty, because she probably would have crashed into something, so recklessly did she reverse out of her spot and accelerate away. The last she saw of Jason Pollack, he was standing by his car, staring after her with an annoyingly unfathomable look on his face.

During her longer than usual drive home—the traffic along Victoria Road was extra heavy, due to an overturned truck—Leah was besieged by mixed emotions.

Regret that she'd now never know what it would be like to be made love to by Jason Pollack, hunk extraordinaire. But relief also that she would never have to face the dilemma of taking off her clothes for him and exposing her scars.

Leah could not bear the thought that he might look at her the way Carl had looked at her that last humiliating time.

But her most overriding emotion was resentment over the man's utter arrogance.

He'd just assumed—because he was the new boss and a billionaire and good looking—that the blonde bimbo receptionist at Beville Holdings would go out with him if he asked. He hadn't even enquired if she had a boyfriend. He probably didn't even care!

Of course, by the time Leah arrived home, worry had set in. Would he find some excuse to sack her? Going to work the next morning suddenly held all kinds of hazards.

'He'll be sorry if he tries to fire me,' she muttered as she went straight to the fridge and grabbed the bottle of Verdelho, which was chilling in the door. A soothing drink was definitely called for tonight. 'He has no idea who he's dealing with here,' she muttered as she reached for the bottle opener. 'No idea at all!'

CHAPTER FOUR

'MR POLLACK WANTS to see you in the function room.'

Leah stiffened in her grey leather office chair.

The moment she had been dreading all day had finally arrived.

He'd said a polite hello to her when he'd arrived this morning with his male PA in tow, a dark-haired, solid fellow in his early thirties. But she hadn't set eyes on either man since. According to Trish at lunchtime, both men had spent all morning going over the sales figures for the past two years, and were planning on spending the afternoon talking to the managers in the marketing division.

By four o'clock, Leah had thought she'd escaped a confrontation over what she'd said in the car park. But it seemed she was wrong.

'Why on earth would he want to see me?' she queried Mandy as she rose reluctantly to her feet.

Mandy shrugged. 'Don't ask me. I'm just the messenger. Maybe he wants to ask you out,' she added with a mischievous twinkle in her eye.

'Very funny.'

The temptation to dash off to the ladies' room to check her appearance was intense. But Leah refused to indulge her vanity, or that secret part of herself that still found Jason Pollack cripplingly attractive. She hadn't stared at him when he arrived this morning, looking suave and smooth in a navy pinstriped suit, crisp white shirt and wine-coloured tie, along with matching kerchief in his breast pocket.

She'd looked at him, as he had looked at her. And said a polite hello, as he had to her. But that was all.

Taking a deep, gathering breath, Leah squared her shoulders and set off down the corridor that ran off the reception area to her right, at the end of which lay a large room that the company used for meetings and functions.

The door was ominously shut, which only increased her nerves. Hopefully, he wouldn't be alone.

Her tap tap on the door sounded firm, despite her hand shaking.

'Come in,' ordered a rich male voice through the door.

His, of course.

Another deep breath as she turned the silver door handle, then pushed open the door.

He was alone, sitting at the boardroom table whose polished length stretched along in front of the tall windows that overlooked the back lawns. That wall faced west and, at this hour, the rays of the low-set sun slanted through the uncurtained sheets of glass, casting his handsome face into shadows, but lighting up his jet-black hair.

Leah hated the way her stomach was churning. Hated *him* for making her feel like this. So vulnerable, and so very foolish.

Jason had steeled himself against her beauty.

What a futile exercise!

She took his breath away again as she entered, her walk as bewitching as the rest of her. She must have once taken ballet lessons, he decided. Or been a model. Her posture was superb. So was the rest of her.

She was wearing pale pink today, a softly feminine dress that wrapped around her slender yet curvy body, covering everything, hiding nothing. Her hair was up, but loosely, a style he'd always liked. As she came closer he could smell her perfume, a tantalising scent that reminded of him faintly of vanilla.

His flesh leapt to attention, making him glad he was sitting at a table.

'You wanted to see me, Mr Pollack?' she said, her green eyes still flashing a frosty dislike at him.

Jason wished he hadn't sent for her now. He was wasting his time here. Torturing himself for nothing. Clearly, he'd misread her yesterday morning. He'd thought he'd seen a spark of mutual attraction in her eyes at the time; thought she'd just been playing a hard-to-get game when she'd walked away and ignored him.

Even after the incident in the car park, his male ego

had managed to momentarily convince himself that her spirited attack was another ploy of the same hard-to-get game. Jason had been the target of many beautiful but ambitious female employees over the last few years, and had become somewhat familiar with their tactics. Some were quite brazen, others more subtle, feigning an initial uninterest, despite their body language telling him otherwise.

During his drive home, Jason had desperately clung to the hope that Ms Johanssen had been one of the latter kind. But as he'd brooded over dinner last night, he had finally come to the more logical conclusion that the girl probably had a steady boyfriend, and was sick to death of being hit on by men. Given how stunning she was, that must happen all the time.

Unfortunately, the thought that Leah Johanssen had a boyfriend, that she might even be living with someone, had not sat well with Jason. The image of her wrapped in some other man's arms that very night had kept him tossing and turning into the wee small hours.

By morning, a bleary-eyed Jason decided not to make a fool of himself with her a second time. He would ignore her from now on, as she had ignored him.

He might have succeeded in this strategy if Bob hadn't told him over afternoon tea that office gossip had the beautiful blonde receptionist of Beville Holdings *without* a current boyfriend.

Which was why Jason had sent for her.

Bad move, as it turned out. All that had been

achieved was a more acute reminder of how devastatingly desirable he found this girl.

As confident as Jason was in his own attractiveness to the opposite sex, there seemed little hope that Leah Johanssen secretly fancied him. Women who secretly fancied men didn't look at them the way she was looking at him at this present moment—like he was a snake that had crawled into her bedroom.

'Please, sit down,' he said to her in curt tones, and indicated the chair opposite him.

'It's ten past four,' she shot back without moving an inch. 'I go home at four thirty.'

Brother, she really had it in for him for whatever reason. He supposed he had come on a bit strong yesterday. Not one of his most subtle invitations.

But someone might like to tell *her* that threatening her new boss with sexual harassment charges wasn't exactly a good career move.

'This won't take long,' he said a bit sharply.

'Very well,' she said, and with a toss of her lovely head, pulled out the chair and sat down, her back ramrod straight, her knees primly together.

Jason gritted his teeth. 'I wanted to apologise to you for what happened in the car park yesterday.'

An apology! It was the last thing Leah was expecting.

'It was arrogant and presumptuous of me to ask you out like that,' he added, using the exact words she'd called him in her mind. 'I'm sorry, Leah. I realise how annoying it must be to be on the end of unwanted attentions and invitations. A girl as beautiful as yourself is probably always getting hit on by men. It must be doubling annoying when it's your new boss at work. Trust me when I say it won't happen again.'

Leah just sat there, totally dumb-struck. Her fear all day had been over his asking her to leave. An apology had not been expected.

Men like him rarely apologised for anything!

'That's all, Leah,' he went on abruptly. 'Thank you for coming.'

As Leah levered herself up out of the chair, she found that her hands were clenched tightly together and her heart was racing like mad. Suddenly, she wanted to say something to him, to soften that hard, tight-lipped expression on his face. But what?

I'm sorry too. I overreacted. I really would have loved to go out to dinner with you last night. But I was afraid you'd make me want to go to bed with you and then I'd have to take off my clothes and you'd see my scars and...

A small shudder rippled down Leah's spine as she realised her thoughts seemed to be spinning out of control.

'I will be calling you in for a proper interview later in the week,' he added matter of factly. 'Only about work matters,' he hastily reassured. 'I hope to interview *all* the employees of Beville Holdings. I trust you won't find that a problem?'

'Not at all, Mr Pollack.' Thank heavens she *sounded* normal!

'Jason, please,' he insisted. 'I always do business on a first-name basis.'

'Jason,' she repeated, the name feeling right for him. A strong name for a strong man. Leah was already beginning to forget why it was she hadn't liked him.

Oh, yes. He'd married an older woman for her money, hadn't he? And now he was single again, a bachelor playboy with a penthouse and a sports car and eyes that kept telling her he wanted to add her to his list of successful takeovers.

His mouth might have apologised, but those burning black eyes kept betraying his true agenda.

Leah hadn't come down in the last shower. Jason Pollack was still interested in her. Men like him didn't back away gracefully. They went after what they wanted with every means at their disposal.

And he had lots of means at his disposal. Money. Position. Power. And more sex appeal than any man had a right to.

Their eyes met and locked, hers struggling to hold on to the coolly haughty expression that she'd adopted since entering the room. She could feel herself melting, surrendering to the heat that radiated from his gaze. Not just her eyes. But her mind. And her whole insides. Melting to mush.

What would it be like, she wondered, to be his girlfriend? To eat with him, and sleep with him. To just *be* with him.

Images filled her mind. Erotic images. Corrupting images.

Just in time she snapped out of it and spun away from him, her hands making fists by her side as she marched towards the door.

'Have a pleasant evening, Leah,' he called after her. 'I'll see you in the morning.'

Jason was still sitting there, mulling over Leah's contradictory body language when Bob came in, holding a couple of plastic folders.

'Well?' Bob said, sitting down in the chair that Leah had just vacated. 'How did it go with the delectable Ms Johanssen?'

'So-so,' Jason replied. Better, actually, than he'd expected. He'd finally seen that spark in her eyes again, the one he'd glimpsed when they'd first met. Though this time, for a few seconds, it had been more than a spark. More of a sizzle.

'Did you ask her out?'

'Not yet.' Despite her momentary lapse, when she'd shown him that she *was* attracted to him, Jason knew he was going to have to be patient.

Not that he felt like being patient. He was still wildly erect under the table, a most unusual state of affairs. The prospect of more nights of tossing and turning was not a pleasant one.

'You have that look in your eye,' Bob said ruefully. 'The one you have when there's some company you're really keen on acquiring. Haven't seen it directed towards a girl before, though.'

'There's a first time for everything,' Jason said,

thinking that he hadn't met a girl quite like this one before.

Karen would have liked Leah, came the sudden and highly unexpected thought.

Karen had always hated women who fell at his feet. Which they had. Most of his life.

Karen had been the first member of the opposite sex who'd initially spurned his advances. And meant it.

It had taken Jason three months of persistence and lots of persuasion before she consented to go out on a date with him. Their age difference had really worried her. Plus what other people thought, especially once she promoted him to CEO of WhizzBiz Electronics.

Jason wondered what it was that worried Leah about him. Something did. He could sense it. His training as a salesman had made him very sensitive to body language.

Maybe she had a hard and fast rule not to mix business with pleasure. Or maybe she'd been burned, like Bob had been last year, and was wary about dating again.

He needed to know more about her. Knowledge was, indeed, power.

'Did you get what I wanted?' he asked Bob.

Bob placed the orange plastic folder on his own lap, then slid the blue one across the table, right into Jason's waiting hands.

Jason's conscience bothered him only slightly as he opened the file and began flicking through the printout of Leah Johanssen's employment record.

I'm the boss, he told himself. It's my right to know the background and qualifications of my employees.

Yeah, especially ones you fancy, his dark side pointed out mockingly.

'I…er…printed out Trish's file as well,' Bob suddenly confessed. 'You know—Jim Matheson's secretary.'

Jason's head snapped up to stare at his PA. 'What on earth for?' He sure as hell didn't fancy *her*.

'I think she's nice. I like her.'

'You do realise she's having an affair with Matheson, don't you?'

'Yeah,' Bob said. 'I sort of gathered that. But Matheson's married, and I'm not. You and I both know he's not going to leave his wife for his secretary. Men like Matheson are serial adulterers. You can bet that Trish isn't the only piece of skirt he's had around here.'

Bob's observation sent the most awful thought into Jason's head. Possibly because he was looking at Leah's resumé at the time.

His stomach contracted fiercely as he saw that she had had no qualifications for her present position when she'd been hired last year. No qualifications for any job, really.

Which meant…what?

Jason had spent a dreadful night last night, imagining her in the arms of some nameless boyfriend. Thinking of her being taken by Jim Matheson on his oversized desk—or on the leather chesterfield in his office—made him feel physically ill!

Logic came to his rescue just in time. Would a girl who'd knocked *him* back so forcefully sleep with a creep like Matheson for some second-rate receptionist job?

Absolutely not. If she'd been that type, she'd have accepted *his* invitation to dinner yesterday.

No, Leah Johanssen was deeper than that. And far more complex. A real mystery woman. Not only did she not have many employment qualifications, she had no past employment record. What had she been doing with her life before starting work here?

'Look, let's get back to business,' he said suddenly, and shoved the pages back into the folder. He'd look at them later, when he had to time to think about nothing but her. 'Give me your first impressions of Beville Holdings as a company.'

Bob leant back in his chair, hooking his right foot over his left knee. 'Well, the problem clearly lies with management, both in sales *and* marketing,' he said. 'But the sales division is by far the worst. Jim Matheson is one slick but rather shifty customer. He'll definitely have to go. And I have no ulterior motive for saying that,' he added swiftly.

'Good. Because no way will I be firing Jim Matheson just yet. Not till *after* I find out what damage he's done. By the way, did you manage to hire someone yesterday to do some speedy market research on all their products?'

'Yep. Should have a report by the end of the week.'

'Great. You'll be coming with me here again tomorrow, by the way. And every day this week.'

'Thank you. And I don't have an ulterior motive for saying that, either. I simply hate staying in the office all by myself, doing nothing but take phone calls. Yesterday was such a bore.'

Jason gave Bob a droll look. Their office was located within Jason's penthouse, with every possible mod con and a heated lap pool a few metres away in which both men swam every day. When he sold WhizzBiz Electronics and became a corporate pirate, Jason decided that renting office space was a waste of time and money. So he'd sold the large home he'd shared with Karen, and bought the top floor of a new skyscraper smack dab in the middle of Sydney.

It had cost him fifteen million dollars, but was probably worth double that now.

'Poor Bob,' he said, with not a trace of sympathy in his voice. 'Any important calls yesterday, by the way?'

'Let's see now. The usual canvassing crap and invitations to stuff you hate. There was *one* rather interesting invite, though. From Joachim Bloom, asking you to a dinner party at his home next Saturday night. I told him I'd get back to him.'

'Joachim Bloom,' Jason repeated thoughtfully. 'Name sounds familiar. Remind me. What does he do?' This was Bob's greatest asset as Jason's PA. He knew everything about everyone who mattered—moneywise—in Australia. Read all the business magazines from cover to cover every month, as well as the business section in every newspaper, every day.

'He's a stockbroker. Old money, but he's managed

to increase his fortune somewhat. Always makes it on to the top two hundred richest in Australia list. A great contact if you want to start taking over strange little companies you know nothing about. He'd probably be able to tell you more about Beville Holdings in one night than we'll be able to find out this entire week.'

'A bit late for that, don't you think?' Jason remarked, toying with the idea of actually saying yes. He wasn't partial to dinner parties, but he'd spent every Saturday night for the past six months with Hilary and suspected he might not want to spend this Saturday night alone. He might be tempted to ring Hilary out of sheer sexual frustration and that would not do. Because it wasn't dark hair he wanted to wake to on the pillow next to him, but blonde.

'Where does Mr Bloom live?' he asked, still thinking of long blonde hair spread out on his pillow.

'Vaucluse.'

'Is there any other address for old money? Okay. Ring him back and accept.'

'Will do,' Bob said as he fished out his phone. 'I have his number and address in here.'

Whilst Bob rang Mr Bloom and accepted the dinner invitation on his behalf, Jason gathered up his papers into his briefcase, including the folder with the file on Leah.

He'd bring her in for that chat soon. But not too soon.

Friday, he decided. By then, he might know how best to handle her.

By then, you're going to be in a bad way, whispered a frustrated voice inside his head.

Just keep busy, he told himself.

'All done,' Bob said. 'You're expected at seven thirty. Saturday night. Black tie.'

'Black tie! Good God, who's coming? The Queen?'

'The best of Sydney society, I suppose.'

'Then why's he asking *me*? I've never been part of that crowd.'

'You want me to ring and cancel?'

'No, no. I'll go. At least the food will be good. And the wine.'

'By the way, he enquired if you had a partner and I said no. Hilary *is* history, isn't she?'

'Absolutely.'

'Good.'

Jason frowned. 'You didn't like Hilary?' As much as Jason didn't make a habit of discussing his personal life with Bob, it was impossible to hide it. Hilary had often dropped in at the penthouse during the day when Bob had been there.

'She was after you for your money,' Bob pronounced, startling Jason.

'But she had money of her own.' Hilary's first husband had been well off, her divorce settlement considerable. She'd owned a very nice house at Harboard Beach, where Jason had spent many weekends with her.

'Some women can never be too rich.'

Jason thought about Hilary's fury when he wouldn't

marry her. She'd claimed to be madly in love with him. But maybe it had never been a matter of love. Jason respected Bob's judgement of character, plus his intuition about people.

'You could be right,' he said. 'Come on. Let's get going. It's been a long day.'

The reception desk was deserted by the time they walked past. Leah's car wasn't in the car park, either. She was gone.

Jason wondered for a moment where she lived. But then he realised he had that detail in his briefcase. He had lots of details about her, not just her address.

Suddenly, he couldn't wait to get home to discover every single one of them.

CHAPTER FIVE

LEAH'S PHONE WAS ringing as she let herself into her apartment. Throwing her bag on to the marble hall stand, she hurried into the living room and swept up the receiver.

'Yes?'

'Hi, there. You sound breathless.'

It was her father.

'I've just walked in the door. Can you hang on till I pour myself a glass of wine?'

'Sure.'

Leah went into the kitchen and poured herself a glass from the bottle of Verdelho that she'd opened the night before, taking it with her and settling into her favourite armchair, which was positioned right next to the phone.

'I'm back,' she said down the line after a couple of refreshing sips.

'Stressful day?'

'No,' she lied. 'I'm just a bit hot and bothered from contending with peak-hour traffic.

'I'm ringing to warn you early in the week that I'm having a dinner party on Saturday night. Nothing too large. Just a dozen or so people.'

'That's all right,' she said. 'I'll stay in my room and read.'

'No, no, I want you to be there, by my side. That's why I'm calling.'

'Oh, Daddy, you know I'm not into that kind of thing any more.'

'Yes, I do know that, more's the pity. You are so very good at making people feel comfortable. Just like your mother was.'

'Mum was marvellous at dinner parties, wasn't she?' Leah said with fond remembrance and a tinge of sadness.

'Yes,' her father agreed. 'And you take after her. The thing is, darling, there's this one gentleman in particular that I've invited. I'd like to sit you next to him at the table. Please come, as a favor to me.'

'Who is he? Not some lecherous old billionaire, Daddy. I have no intention of spending an entire evening, slapping his hands away under the table.'

Her father laughed. 'Would I do that to you?'

'You can be quite ruthless where money is concerned. So who is this mystery dinner guest, exactly?'

'Someone who has everything, except me as his broker.'

'If you won't tell me his name, my guess is he *is* old and lecherous.'

'Not at all!' her father denied.

Leah rolled her eyes. Most of her father's male clients were over sixty, multi-millionaires who still thought they were God's gift to women, despite their balding heads and pot bellies.

'Promise me he's not too revolting.'

'He's not at all revolting. Honestly.'

'I suppose you'll want me to doll myself up.'

'You could never look anything but beautiful, Leah. But, yes, it's black tie.'

Leah sighed. She'd once loved black tie parties. Loved dressing up to the nines. Loved wearing designer dresses and diamonds.

Somehow, such dos seemed pretentious now, filled with pompous, privileged people who had no idea how the other half lived.

But she loved her father and it would be churlish of her to refuse. He rarely asked anything of her.

So come next Saturday night, she'd doll herself up and sit next to this rich old codger and do her best to charm him.

'Okay,' she agreed.

'Darling, that's wonderful. I do appreciate it. And you'll enjoy yourself, I'm sure. I'm having the food done by that catering company your mother always hired. More than a dozen people is a bit much to expect Mrs B. to cook for. And I'm going to open some of my best wines.'

'Heavens!' This potential client must be very rich indeed.

'The invitations are for seven thirty, but I presume you'll already be here long before then.'

Leah spent most Saturdays at Westmead Hospital, visiting the children's wards and doing what she could to bring a little joy into the lives of the poor kids there, especially the ones in the cancer ward. During her own long rehabilitation in that same hospital, she'd taken to wandering the corridors, discovering that there were plenty of people worse off than herself. It had been the children, however, who had affected her most deeply. Poor little mites.

Yet so brave. Sometimes she felt quite ashamed of herself when she visited them. They rarely complained, even when all their hair had fallen out. She knew she'd be devastated if all her hair fell out. Yet she was ashamed of a few miserable scars that didn't even show.

She usually left around four—the children were getting tired by then, anyway—and drove straight to Vaucluse, arriving at her father's around five.

'I'll try to make it home by four,' she told him. 'It's so long since I've dolled myself up to this degree, it might take a while. Do you want me to help with the flowers? Or the table setting?'

'No. I don't want you to do a thing. Just look beautiful.'

Leah winced. That was what Carl always said to her when they had a party. She had liked it at the time but had since read an awful shallowness into the comment, as though she had nothing more to offer than her physical beauty.

Which, as it turned out, had been correct where Carl

was concerned. He hadn't valued her intelligence. Or her joy of life. Or her soul. His love for her had been as skin deep as her supposed beauty.

Leah sighed. And what if I were ugly, Daddy? she felt like asking. What if I had no hair? Would you still want me to co-host your dinner party? Was her father's love for her tainted by her looks as well?

'I have to go cook myself something, Daddy,' she said abruptly. 'All this talk of food has made me hungry.'

'You do that, daughter. See you Saturday. Love you.'

And he hung up.

Leah gripped the phone for a few seconds before dropping it back into its cradle. He *did* love her. She knew he did.

But then, he was her father.

No other man had ever really loved her, she accepted painfully. Not any of her silly boyfriends. And Carl, least of all.

True love encompassed more than sexual attraction. It was deeply caring, and strongly committed, and totally unconditional. True love didn't abandon you when things got tough. True love was like a rock.

And true love, Leah realised ruefully, was not be found in a pair of dark eyes that sizzled and smouldered whenever they looked at her. She knew exactly what Jason Pollack wanted from her, and it wasn't commitment and caring. He didn't want to be her true love, just her lover.

The man had to be resisted.

Not an easy task, she conceded as she recalled what had happened to her this afternoon.

How long, she wondered, before he made his next move? And he would. She was sure of it.

Maybe it was time for her to move on. To resign and find herself another job. She shouldn't have the same trouble as she had the first time. She had experience now.

Yes, Leah decided. That was what she had to do. Resign.

She'd type out the letter at work tomorrow. And when Jason Pollack brought her in for that interview, she'd give it to him.

CHAPTER SIX

BY FOUR O'CLOCK Friday, Leah had worked herself up into a state. Jason hadn't called her in for that interview, though everyone else seemed to have trundled down to the function room over the past three days. Today, all the reps had been brought in off the road, going in for their interviews one by one, then stopping by her desk afterwards to tell her how absolutely fantastic the new boss was, and that their jobs were safe.

Peter, of course, was very relieved, though he confided to Leah that he hoped someone eventually told Mr Pollack—or his offsider—how hopeless their field sales manager was. Shelley had totally botched up their territories, he'd complained. As well as their country runs.

By four twenty-five, Leah had given up hope that she was going to have the opportunity this week to hand in her resignation personally.

Part of her was relieved. She hadn't been looking forward to another confrontation with Jason Pollack, which is what it would have become.

On another level, she wished it was over. Now, she would think about that infernal man all weekend.

Leah started tidying up her desk, ready to leave at four thirty, when Trish showed up, looking flushed and excited.

'I'm not going down to the pub for drinks tonight,' she announced. 'Sorry.'

'That's all right,' Leah returned. 'I'm going straight home tonight, anyway.'

She'd been afraid the new and much-lauded boss might show up at the pub, since he didn't stand on ceremony. The last thing Leah wanted was to be with him in a semi-social situation. It had been bad enough, greeting him politely every morning and afternoon this week, as well as during the day when he walked past on the way to the factory, or the canteen, or wherever he'd been going. He always smiled at her, and it was impossible not to smile back. Her mouth simply didn't obey her when he was around. Neither did her eyes. She hadn't ogled him, exactly. But it had been a close call.

'Where are you off to instead?' she asked Trish.

'You'll never guess. Bob's asked me out.'

'Bob who? Oh, you mean Bob, the right-hand man.'

'Yes.' Trish beamed.

'That's great, Trish,' Leah said with a warm smile. 'Bob seems nice.'

'He is. *Very.* Jim's most put out, but I'd already told him it was over between us. He's gone off home in a huff.'

Leah frowned. 'I didn't see him leave.'

'He went out the side door.'

'Has Mr Pollack left the same way?' she asked hopefully.

'No. He's still in the function room with Bob. And you'd better start calling him Jason. He hates being called Mr Pollack.'

Leah sighed. 'I won't have to worry about that for much longer, Trish. I've decided to resign.'

'What? But *why*?' Trish looked upset.

'I think it's time I tried something a little more challenging.'

'Oh, dear, I'm going to miss you terribly. Couldn't you possibly find something more challenging here? Bob told me Jason is planning a brand new advertising campaign to get sales moving. You might be able to help with that.'

'I don't think so, Trish,' Leah said, switching on the answering machine, then bending down to get her handbag from where it was sitting on the floor under the desk.

'You haven't resigned yet, have you?'

'What's this about resigning?'

Leah's head snapped up to find Jason striding towards them, his handsome face not smiling at her *this* time. Bob was a few steps behind, *his* face full of smiles as he looked at Trish.

'Leah. She says she needs something more challenging,' Trish said before Leah could assemble her thoughts, and her defences. 'You could find her something in marketing, Jason, couldn't you?'

The boss's darkly frustrated eyes went to Leah's. 'I would not dream of forcing Ms Johannsen into doing anything she didn't want to do,' he replied, the use of her last name showing he was not pleased by her decision. 'But if she wishes, yes, I'm sure something could be arranged. I would hate to lose such a valued employee.'

'See?' Trish said happily.

'I hear you and Bob are going out to dinner tonight,' Jason directed toward Trish. 'Why don't you two run along and leave me to have a private word with Leah? I was meaning to speak to her today, but time simply ran out on me.'

Leah hated the feeling of people talking around her. Hated the feeling of losing control of her own life.

She didn't want to have a private word with this man. She didn't want to have a private *anything* with him.

But Bob was swift to obey his boss's command, and soon they were alone together. Though thankfully, not for long. The office staff kept going by on their way out, saying a polite cheerio to Jason, then calling out to Leah that they'd see her later down at the pub.

Finally, however, the trail of people ceased and Leah was forced to face her nemesis, alone.

'You go somewhere for drinks on a Friday night?' he asked from where he was still standing on the other side of the desk. Thank goodness.

'Usually. But not tonight.' She stood up, her handbag at the ready to make a quick exit.

'Why not?'

'Trish won't be there. I usually sit with her and I don't like to go alone.'

'I could take you,' came his immediate offer.

'Absolutely not!'

'Why not?'

'I don't like to be the object of office gossip.'

'But you're resigning. Or so you say,' he added, a slightly cynical edge creeping into his voice.

Leah bristled. 'I always mean what I say. I am resigning, and there's nothing you can say or do to stop me.'

He stared at her, his head cocking slightly on one side. 'Why are you afraid of me?'

Leah stiffened. 'I am not afraid of you.'

'Oh, yes, you are. Yet you shouldn't be. I don't mean you any harm, Leah. I like you. No, that's a rather colossal understatement. I'm extremely attracted to you. I'd love to take you out.'

'You'd love to take me to bed,' she snapped, the words tripping off her tongue with a flash of venom.

His smile was her undoing. Because it was so damned honest.

'That, too,' he admitted. 'But is that such a crime? Look at it from my angle, Leah,' he went on persuasively. 'I'm a single man. You're a single woman. Without a current boyfriend, I'm told. Yes, I also admit to asking around the office about you. That's what men do when they're interested in a woman. And I am very interested in you.'

'Why?' she threw at him.

He looked rattled for a moment.

'Why not?'

'Do *you* have a current girlfriend?' she quizzed him.

'No.'

'Now why do I find that hard to believe?' she scoffed.

'I did have a girlfriend till recently. We split up a couple of weeks ago.'

How typical, she thought. Out with the old and in with the new. Men like him were never long without a woman on their arm, and in their bed. Good-looking women. Never plain ones.

'Come out with me tonight, Leah. Get to know me. I'm not what you think.'

But you *are*, Jason's conscience jeered. You're not interested in a real relationship with this girl. You don't want to marry her, or have children with her. She's dead right about you. You just want her in your bed, at your beck and call.

A measure of guilt flooded in with this admission. But it wasn't as strong as his desire, a desire that had become almost obsessive this past week. He'd had extreme difficulty putting his mind to the takeover of this company, his thoughts constantly distracted by her physical nearness. He kept making excuses to walk by reception, just to see her, and to reassure himself that the chemistry between them was mutual.

It was. He *knew* it was.

He'd delayed interviewing her, in the hope of calming her concerns about him. But that hadn't worked. She was going to resign.

Exasperation joined his desperation. 'If you're not afraid of me and you're going to resign, then there's nothing to stop you coming out with me tonight. *Is* there?' he ground out.

'Maybe I just don't like you,' she snapped back. 'Or hasn't that occurred to your highness?'

Jason's teeth clenched hard in his jaw. Damn, but if that desk wasn't between them, he'd sweep her into his arms and kiss that saucy mouth of hers into total silence.

As it was, all he could do was glower at her.

She glowered right back.

If only he knew *why* she was fighting the chemistry between them. Her employment file hadn't helped him all that much. She was still one big mystery.

The arrival of the cleaners gave Jason the opportunity he was looking for.

'We need to talk,' he pronounced firmly. 'In private. Come with me.'

Leah threw a frantic glance at the two cleaners who steadfastly ignored her. Other than making a scene, she had no option but to do what he asked.

Grabbing her handbag, she followed him down to the function room, thinking to herself that it would be ages before the cleaners got down there. She would be alone with him for far too long without any hope of interruption.

'This is all nonsense,' he declared after he banged the door shut behind her. 'Your resigning is nonsense. *That* is nonsense,' he said, waving an impatient hand in her direction.

'I have no idea what you're talking about,' she retorted, though she suspected he was referring to the way she was clutching her handbag in front of her, like a shield.

He began to pace about the room, raking his hands through his hair and muttering to himself. When he reached the far side of the boardroom table, he ground to a halt, his eyes stabbing across the room at her.

'What in hell's wrong with you?' he demanded to know. 'You say one thing, but your eyes keep telling me a different story. Are you or are you not attracted to me?'

Leah swallowed. A direct interrogation was the last approach she'd expected. She'd been worried he might do something more physical.

'Don't give me some bulldust answer, Leah. Tell me the truth.'

She drew herself up as tall as she could, doing her best to maintain her dignity, whilst all the while thinking he was devastatingly attractive when he was angry. The passion in his eyes and his face was extremely flattering, and incredibly seductive. Because it was all for *her.*

'You are a very handsome man,' she said, shaken by the dizzying waves of desire which started washing through her.

'Handsome is as handsome does,' he returned sharply. 'What I want to know is do you want me as I want you, damn it?'

'I…I…' She could not go on. Could not say another word. Not yes. Or no. Nothing.

Her mouth had gone bone dry. Her mind went blank.

Her inability to answer thrilled Jason. Then aroused him. He had to touch her. Had to kiss her.

When he strode around the table towards her, her eyes blinked wide, her lips falling slightly apart.

But she didn't turn and run.

Jason didn't know why she'd been afraid of him. Or if she still was. But he was beyond caring. All that mattered at that moment was what her eyes kept telling him.

She was standing there, waiting for him, wanting him as he wanted her.

Disposing of that silly handbag took less than a second. Pulling her into his arms even less.

He groaned as his mouth took possession of hers, his arms folding her close, then closer still. Technique seemed unimportant in the face of the emotion that threatened to overwhelm him. Triumph mingled with the most intoxicating pleasure. The kiss went on, and on, and on. Not foreplay, but an experience in itself, satisfying him with the way her body melted against his, her soft moans music to his ears.

Jason knew, long before his head lifted, that she was his. He didn't need to rush things now. A quickie in this office was not what he'd been thinking about and craving all week. He wanted her in his bed. Tonight. All night.

And that was only for starters.

'You are so beautiful,' he whispered against her hair, his arms holding her close, close enough to feel the instant stiffening of her muscles.

What had he done wrong now?

She wrenched out of his arms, her face flushed, her eyes tormented as she stumbled back from him.

'I'm sorry,' she choked out. 'But I can't do this. No, don't touch me again!' she threw at him when he took a step toward her. 'If you do, I'll scream.'

He froze, his body as frustrated at his mind. What on earth was the matter with this girl?

'You're crazy, do you know that?'

'Yes,' she replied with a funny little laugh. 'Yes. I think I must be.' And she bent to scoop up her bag from where he'd dropped it on the floor.

Panic filled his heart that she would go and he would never see her again. Without thinking of the consequences, he reached out and grabbed her on the arm.

'You can't just leave without explaining yourself.'

The emotional distress in her eyes was instantly replaced with a defiant fury. 'I don't have to explain myself to you,' she spat as she shook his hand away. 'I'm going home now and I strongly suggest you don't try to stop me.'

His mouth opened to demand she tell him if she would be here on Monday. But she was already out the door, fleeing from him like he was the devil himself.

Jason had never felt so helpless before. Or more frustrated. Logic told him to just let her go. Clearly, the girl had some serious problem where men were concerned.

But then he remembered how she'd felt in his arms and he knew that he could not follow his own advice.

This wasn't over yet. Not by a long shot.

CHAPTER SEVEN

AS JASON NEARED the address he'd found in Leah's employment file, he tried telling himself once again that this was not a good idea.

But it was no use. Common sense was not directing his actions, the same way it hadn't when he'd bought Beville Holdings.

On that occasion, he'd felt compelled by a silly dream. This time, his dark side seemed to have taken complete control, driving him on to pursue Leah Johanssen tonight, regardless of her earlier rejection.

No, not rejection. More of a defection. When he'd been kissing her, she'd very definitely been kissing him back. But something had happened to make her freeze up, and flee. Some thought had come into her head. Some fear. Underneath her panic, she had still wanted him. He was sure of it.

Or so he'd like to convince himself.

The clock on the dash said it was nearing eight as he turned the corner into her street. The battle between his conscience and his desires had already taken a couple of angst-filled hours, but, in the end, his desires had won, hands down.

And here he was in Gladesville, every pore in his body aching with the need to have her in his arms once more. The effects of the cold shower he'd had when he'd first arrived home that evening had long dissipated. Wanting her had become a need almost as essential as breathing.

He would not rest until that need was satisfied. He would use every means at his disposal to win her. Every method of persuasion. Every tactic. Every weapon.

A measure of surprise hit Jason as he slid his car into the curb outside the number that housed his prey.

This was not what he expected.

He'd known Gladesville had gradually moved from strictly working class to a more trendy suburb over the past decade or so. But most of the apartment blocks in the area were still plain brick buildings, built half a century ago, unlike the cream, cement-rendered, very modern building he was currently staring at.

On top of that, this building sat directly opposite Sydney's inner harbour.

Waterfront addresses of any kind in Sydney were prized, and added heaps to the price of any apartment. Jason could also see a smartly dressed security man seated in the large, well-lit foyer, which indicated an exclusiveness associated with top-line addresses.

No way could Leah afford to rent such a place on her own. Not on the salary Beville Holdings paid her, anyway. Maybe she shared with a couple of other working girls.

Jason hadn't thought of Leah as having flatmates, let alone a security man barring his way in.

Suddenly, his showing up here like this seemed a very bad idea. And doomed to failure.

Yet going home with his tail between his legs didn't appeal, either.

Damn, but he wished he knew more about this girl. Asking around about her at Beville Holdings hadn't revealed anything worthwhile, other than her apparent lack of a boyfriend. Her employment file hadn't provided much help, either.

Her past history was chock full of holes. He would love to know what she'd done with her life from the time she'd left school till she started work at Beville Holdings last year at the age of twenty-five. According to her resumé, not a thing, other than a brief creative writing course.

Maybe she'd lived at home whilst she'd tried to make it as a novelist, wherever home was. The section on her job application form where she was supposed to list her next of kin had been left suspiciously blank.

Maybe she was an orphan, or a runaway. Maybe she'd been a very bad girl at one stage in her life, doing things you didn't include on your resumé.

No…no, a bad girl would not have bolted when her wealthy boss came on to her. A bad girl would have done anything he wanted.

He didn't really want her to be a bad girl, anyway,

did he? Not down deep. He'd felt nauseous at the thought of her having sex with Jim Matheson. He liked her not having fallen at his feet. He liked her character and spirit. What he didn't like was not knowing what had made her run from the obvious chemistry between them. It didn't make sense. It was crazy, like he'd said.

What to do, Jason? Go home, or take a chance and ring her? He had her phone number, just as he had her address.

His cell phone was in his hands in no time flat. Because there really wasn't any contest, was there? He could not go home without at least trying to find out the truth.

Leah tied the sash on her silk bathrobe before carrying the glass of Chablis back into her kitchen and pouring the lukewarm contents down the sink.

Now what? she wondered.

When Leah had first arrived home from work, she hadn't been able to settle to anything. Eating was out of the question. She was too churned up to eat. She'd paced her apartment for ages, calling herself all sorts of names, from a fool to a coward. She'd taken herself out on to her balcony and stared at the water for ages, but it hadn't soothed her, as it usually did.

In the end, she'd run herself a hot bath, poured herself a glass of wine and lain there in the perfumed bubbles for ages, clasping the undrunk Chablis till it went warm and the water was stone cold, all the while trying desperately not to think of how it had felt when Jason kissed her.

Futile exercise.

It was all she could think about.

The sensations of his mouth on hers had been amazing. She'd never felt anything like it. She'd been in heaven. Even so, her silly fears had finally overridden her pleasure, forcing her to cut and run.

Jason had called her crazy and she'd agreed with him. It seemed crazy to turn her back on something so pleasurable, and which promised even more pleasure in the future.

It felt even crazier now that the heat of the moment had subsided and she could think about the situation more rationally.

How long was she going to let her fear of humiliation and rejection spoil everything? Did she honestly plan never to have sex ever again in her entire life?

Leah sighed. She'd made a right mess of things with Jason this afternoon. Now she really would have to resign first thing on Monday morning. There was no other way out. She could not possibly work with the man after this.

'I shouldn't have let him kiss me,' she muttered as she walked into the kitchen to get herself a fresh glass of wine. But, oh, it had felt so good.

The phone ringing brought a burst of frustration.

'Botheration!' she exclaimed. She didn't want to talk to anyone. Especially her father. And she couldn't think who else it might be at this hour on a Friday night.

Hopefully, it was a carpet-cleaning company, trying to get some business with some cold calls.

Not that they would have any success. Her carpets didn't need cleaning.

Leah hurried into the living room, put down her glass of wine then swept up her mobile phone.

'Yes?' she said rather impatiently.

'Leah?'

Leah's heart stopped. It was him. Her soon-to-be ex-boss. Jason Pollack. Driving her crazy some more.

Her heart lurched back to life, thudding noisily behind her ribs whilst her head whirled with conflicting emotions. Anger fired her blood. But there was excitement, too.

He wasn't going to take no for an answer. What a perversely thrilling thought!

'How did you get my phone number?' she demanded, her voice literally shaking.

'I looked it up in your employment file.'

Leah sucked in sharply. How utterly conscienceless he was. Like Carl.

'I know I shouldn't have,' he went on immediately in urgent tones. 'I know you could really charge me with sexual harassment this time. But I just couldn't sleep tonight without finding out what I did wrong earlier.'

Leah could not help but be impressed by his seemingly sincere tone. Maybe he wasn't as conscienceless as she imagined.

'You didn't do anything wrong,' she conceded tautly. Except perhaps be a far-too-good kisser.

'Then what happened? One moment you were right there with me. The next you were out the door. Were you worried I might push things further right then and there?'

Leah shuddered with the image of his lifting her up on to that boardroom table, then pushing her skirt up to expose her scarred thigh. 'In a way…'

'But I wouldn't have. Not with those cleaners wandering about. I wouldn't have done that, Leah.'

Wouldn't he? She wasn't so sure, either of him or of herself. The sexual heat they generated together was extremely powerful.

She'd wanted him. She still wanted him, despite knowing what kind of man he was. Maybe not totally conscienceless. But arrogant and ruthless. A taker.

'Tell me what the problem is, Leah,' he insisted down the line, his tone bewitchingly gentle and understanding. 'I get the feeling it's not me personally. It's something else, isn't it?'

Leah wanted to tell him. She really did. Yet still she hesitated. Because if Jason didn't react the way Carl had, then she would be left with no defences against him at all.

She wouldn't be able to resist the man if he still wanted her, despite her scars. She would be his for the taking.

Leah hated the thought of becoming some rich man's sexual puppet. She'd battled over the past two years to throw off the legacy of her pampered past and find purpose in her life. To take control of her own destiny. To become a true adult.

She would not throw away her new sense of independence and self-worth because her body wanted this man to make love to it.

If she was going to have an affair with Jason—and she really wanted to—it would be on her terms, not his. And only if she truly believed her scars didn't bother him.

Leah decided then and there not to tell Jason about the accident over the phone. She would not give him the chance to become used to the idea of her being scarred. She would *show* him. Without warning. And she would watch his eyes.

His eyes would tell her all she needed to know.

'I think we need to talk,' she said abruptly. 'Could you come over to my place?'

Jason did a double take at his end of the line. But he pulled himself together quickly. He'd never been a man to look a gift horse in the mouth.

'When?' he asked.

'How about now—tonight?'

His heart leapt. So did something else.

'I'll be right up.'

'*What?* You mean…' Leah ran across her living room, through the open glass doors and out on to her balcony, almost dropping the phone when she leant over the railing.

Directly below sat his blue sports car, the driver's door swinging open as she peered down.

He climbed out, his phone still clamped to his ear.

He was casually dressed, the charcoal business suit

he'd been wearing at work now replaced by bone chinos and a dark open-necked shirt that shimmered faintly purple under the street light. His dark hair shone as well, indicating a recent shower.

Even from that distance Leah experienced a squishy feeling in her stomach as she stared down at him.

'I got your address from your employment file as well,' he confessed drily as he banged the car door shut, then glanced up the three floors towards her balcony. When their eyes connected, Leah swallowed.

'You're a wicked man,' she choked out.

'You're a very beautiful woman,' he replied smoothly.

Leah's chest tightened. So they were back to that again. Her so-called beauty. This time, however, she wasn't going to run away. She was going to see what Jason was made of.

'I'll tell Keith to let you come up,' she said abruptly, and swung away from the railing. 'I'm in apartment 3a.'

Unnecessary information, she realised after she let the doorman know the name of her imminent visitor. Jason already knew her address. And her phone number. And whatever else was in her resumé.

Though that wasn't much. She'd protected her true identity and her past from prying eyes at work.

Jason knew nothing of her marriage to Carl, or that she was an heiress in her own right.

How much should I tell him? she wondered, and then worried. A man who had once married for money should possibly be kept in the dark about her wealth.

But how could she explain this apartment?

She would have to tell him something.

Her doorbell ringing sent Leah into a spin. She should not have just stood there, dithering. She should have gone and put some clothes on. To answer her door with nothing on but her bathrobe was brazen in the extreme.

Yet she wasn't brazen. Not at all!

She was, however, determined to be master of her own destiny. Given that, there was little point in dressing now, Leah decided.

Tightening the sash around her waist, she scooped in a deep breath, then walked with a renewed sense of composure towards the door.

CHAPTER EIGHT

JASON COULD NOT believe how nervous he felt as he waited for Leah to answer her doorbell. Like a schoolboy on his first real date.

Once she'd invited him up, he hadn't had the patience to take the lift. Instead, he'd charged up the three flights of stairs, taking several steps at a time, arriving at her floor with his blood hot and his heart galloping like a racehorse in the final furlong of the Melbourne Cup.

The door finally opened, and his pounding heart skidded to a halt.

During his swinging single years—before he'd met and married Karen—Jason had had apartment doors opened to him by sexily dressed women. And scantily clad women. Once, he'd even been met at the door by a stark naked woman.

But none had affected him as powerfully as the sight of Leah Johannsen, encased in a Japanese-style robe that was almost as exquisite as she was.

The fact that she was braless beneath the red silk kimono was swiftly all too evident. So was the fact that she was either as excited as he was…or very cold.

Given it was summer, he didn't think the latter was an option. Not a calming thought.

Jason suddenly didn't know where to look. Certainly not at her rock-like nipples. Or into her seductive green eyes. Or that softly luscious mouth whose lipstick he could still taste on his own lips.

He found himself staring over her shoulder into the main living area of her apartment, noting its spaciousness, and style. Nothing bargain basement in there. Or shared. Jason knew, without being told, that Leah didn't have any flatmates. She lived here alone. The only unknown was how she could afford it.

A dark suspicion invaded his mind. Maybe she didn't always live here alone. Maybe someone else paid the rent, then paid her the occasional visit. Maybe that was where the problem lay with her. She already had a rich lover and wasn't free to take another.

'Come in,' she said throatily, taking a step back and waving him inside.

As he moved past her, Jason glanced down at her bare but beautiful feet with their scarlet painted toes, thinking to himself that he would have those feet wound around him before this night was out, regardless.

His heart jolted back into life, thudding with wicked purpose.

'This is a pretty swanky place,' he heard himself

saying as he moved across the plush, sable-coloured carpet towards the elegant seating arrangement in the centre of the room. 'How on earth can you afford it on your salary?'

He turned to find her regarding him with an expression that made him feel ashamed of his suspicion.

'I can't,' she replied coldly. 'I own this apartment. I bought it with some money that was left to me a couple of years ago.'

Jason's eyebrows lifted. Had to have been a reasonably sizeable inheritance. 'I see,' he said.

'I doubt it,' she snapped, and walked over to pick up a glass of wine, which was sitting on one of the two side tables flanking the rich cream sofa.

'Forgive me if I don't offer you a drink just yet,' she said, and gulped down the wine. 'I need a little Dutch courage here,' she added as she placed the glass back where it came from.

Before he could open his mouth to ask her what was going on, her hands went to the sash around her waist.

Shock had him swallowing. As much as he wanted this girl, he didn't want her to strip off in front of him like...like some cheap slut. He wanted to take her in his arms and kiss as he had before. He wanted to hear her moan, feel her melt against him. He wanted to make love to her, damn it!

But she didn't undo the ties. Instead, she gripped them tightly in one hand whilst her other hand moved down to splay across her stomach, like she was holding it in. Suddenly, she shoved her right leg forward, the action parting the robe right up to mid-thigh, but no further. All Jason could see was her leg. A very beautifully shaped leg with a nice calf muscle and slender ankle.

But just a leg.

Leah watched his eyes like a hawk watches its prey. Watched them and waited.

But the only emotion she could find in his startled gaze was surprise, followed by a weird kind of relief.

Was the man blind? Surely he could see the scars. Surely!

But he didn't seem to notice them.

When she looked down, Leah saw that the worst of the scars were still hidden by the robe. In her efforts to maintain her dignity, she'd kept the darned thing shut too far.

'*Now* can you see them?' she said, thrusting her leg out a bit further, at the same time pointing her toe and unbending her knee.

He just blinked. Nothing more. Just a blink, followed by a small frown of bewilderment.

'Yes,' he eventually replied. 'I can see them.'

'*And?*' she ground out, totally thrown by his reaction. He had to be pretending. Had to be. No one could look at those ugly white ridges and not feel some repulsion. *She* was repulsed, and she'd lived with them for two years.

'Is this what the problem is?' he questioned her quietly, his gaze no longer on her leg, but on her face. 'Those little marks on your thigh?'

'Little marks?' she practically screamed at him as she pulled her leg back in and wrapped the robe back defensively around it. 'They're not little marks. They're *scars*. Horrible, hideous, huge scars. Stop pretending they aren't.'

He seemed taken aback. 'Show them to me again,' he said. 'Maybe I didn't see them correctly.'

Jason saw the horror in her face at his suggestion, sympathy filling his heart as he remembered how Karen had felt about her mastectomy scars. He'd had a lot of trouble convincing his wife that he still found her a desirable woman without her breasts. She would cover her scarred chest all the time.

His heart sank as the reality of this situation sank in. This girl was far too vulnerable for him to use as he'd been going to use her. No point in his pussy-footing around with his own less-than-honourable intentions. He had to be straight with himself. His plan had been a rather callous seduction tonight, followed by a strictly sexual affair.

Some women could cope with that kind of thing. But Leah wasn't one of them.

'They're not so bad, Leah,' Jason said with a soft sigh. 'I didn't even notice them at first.'

'Yeah, right,' she said, her arms lifting to wrap around herself.

Jason just stood there, not sure what to say and do. 'So what happened?' he finally asked.

'Do you really want to know?' she threw at him.

'Yes,' he returned firmly.

'I was in a car accident. Two years ago.'

'And?'

'And I don't really want to talk about it. Look, you don't have to stay and make sympathetic noises. I can see by your body language that you'd rather just cut and run. I understand. Truly. I've been there, done that, with another man just like you. I mean…you only want physical perfection, don't you? Not damaged goods.'

Jason stared at her. She was right. And she was wrong. He didn't give a damn about the scars. He still found her incredibly beautiful and desirable.

But he did want to cut and run, before he was tempted to totally forget his conscience and exploit her vulnerabilities for all they were worth. Some man—some contemptible bastard—had done a right number on her at some stage. Probably told her she was ugly now, or some such stupid thing.

'Who was it, Leah?' he demanded to know.

Her green eyes flashed at him. 'Who was what?'

'The man who made you so self-conscious about your scars?'

'My husband, if you must know.'

'Husband!' So that was what she'd been doing all those years. She'd been married.

'Yes. I was married,' she confirmed sharply. 'Once. But never again, I assure you.'

Her bitter assurance was a temptation in itself. After all, he didn't want to get married again, either.

Not because he'd been betrayed. But because he'd loved too much.

That was what *this* girl needed. To be loved the way he'd loved Karen. Jason knew he didn't have that kind of love left in him any more. But maybe somewhere there was some man who did, some really decent guy who would show Leah that her life wasn't over because of one man's shallowness and cruelty.

If he left her alone, she might find that man. She'd just be wasting her time with him.

When he came towards her, alarm filled her face and her arms tightened around herself.

'What…what are you doing?' she said, stumbling back against the sofa when he reached out to cup her face.

'I'm going to kiss you goodbye,' he said, and planted a soft peck on her forehead. 'Not because of your scars, Leah. I won't let you believe that, because it isn't true. I still think you are the most beautiful, most desirable girl I have ever met. But because you deserve someone a lot better than me in your life.'

Her eyes swam with tears as she gazed up at him. 'You…you don't want me any more.'

His heart actually twisted. 'I want you now more than ever.'

'Then show me,' she begged him.

'God, but you're making it hard.'

'I don't want you to go,' she sobbed, and suddenly wrapped her arms around his back, pulling him tightly against her. 'Please. Please don't go. Stay with me to-night.'

He jerked back to stare down into her tear-stained face and pleading eyes.

'You don't mean that.'

'I do. I do.'

The desperation in her voice was an even more persuasive force than the feel of her body pressed up to his. And that was pretty persuasive.

How could he possibly leave her now? Her self-confidence would be shattered for ever if he did.

But even as his mouth began to descend, Jason vowed to himself that tonight was all there would be. One night, he would give her. And himself. He wasn't that much of a hypocrite that he didn't recognise he was going to get something out of this, too.

But by morning he would be gone. Gone from her bed and her life. Otherwise, he wouldn't be able to live with himself.

CHAPTER NINE

HE STILL WANTS me, Leah cried to herself as his mouth took passionate possession of hers.

No peck on the forehead this time. A real kiss, deep and hungry, flooding her with waves of desire, so hot and strong she thought she might faint with them. She could not get enough of his mouth, but especially his tongue. Each time it slipped past her teeth, she wanted to keep it there, a prisoner of her own passion.

'No, don't stop,' she cried aloud when his head finally lifted.

His wry laughter was reassuring.

'I don't think you have to worry about my stopping, beautiful,' he told her as he swept her up into his arms. 'I presume this is the way to your bedroom,' he added as he carried her down the only hallway in her apartment.

She didn't reply. She was too busy looking up at him with wildly adoring eyes. How handsome he was. Perfect in every way, from his dark, deeply set eyes to his incredibly sexy mouth.

When her right hand lifted to touch his full bottom lip, his step faltered, his eyes glittering as they dropped to hers.

'If you keep doing that,' he growled, 'and looking at me like that, I won't be able to control myself.'

'I don't want you to control yourself,' she confessed.

His four-letter word shocked her, but only because it excited her beyond her own control.

She almost told him yes, yes, that's what I want you to do to me. Nothing gentle. Nothing romantic. I want it rough and wild.

'Tell me you can't possibly get pregnant tonight,' came his gruff request.

'I can't possibly get pregnant tonight,' she replied obediently, whilst thinking to herself that it *was* unlikely. Her period had only just finished a couple of days ago.

But, in truth, she didn't care. She didn't care about anything but having him make mad passionate love to her.

'Thank goodness,' Jason muttered darkly as he carried her into her bedroom.

The room was exactly what he would have expected her bedroom to look like. Soft and pretty and feminine, with pale cream walls and a buttery cream carpet. The brass bed resting against the far wall looked like a genuine antique. High, but not that wide, with a cream lace valance, cream satin quilt and a mound of matching satin and lace pillows resting against the bedhead. The brass-based lamps sitting on the two antique bedside chests were exquisite, their cream shades edged with long drops of crystal. They were both switched on, casting soft circles of lights over the bed.

The realisation that he would soon be on that bed with Leah did little to help Jason's uncharacteristic lack of control. He'd never been like this with Hilary. Or even Karen, whom he'd loved. Truthfully, he hadn't *ever* been like this.

How on earth am I going to make this good for her? he worried as he carried Leah across the room. Already he was painfully erect, his blood charging through his veins at the rate of knots. He ached to throw her on to that virginal-looking quilt and just do it. Without foreplay. Without anything. Just straight into her. Pounding away.

'Do you have *anything* on under that robe?' he asked thickly as he lowered her to her feet beside the bed.

She shook her head and swayed against him, the silken tips of her breasts connecting with his stomach.

He sucked in sharply. 'Hell, Leah, I hope you meant it about wanting me to lose control. Because I'm losing it right now.'

'Good,' she said, her glittering green eyes not in any way shy, but suddenly surprisingly bold.

Jason needed no further encouragement.

He yanked the robe back off her shoulders, not bothering with the ties. But when he dragged it down her arms, the damned thing stopped at her waist, trapping her arms by her sides and leaving him staring at the most provocative and perfect breasts he had ever seen.

Lusciously full, they were. High-set, not heavy, with large aureoles and the pinkest, pointiest nipples.

He had to touch them. Tug at them. Taste them.

'Oh, Leah, Leah,' he groaned as he scooped her up and laid her down in the middle of her quilt, his eyes hot on her as he straightened to stand at the side of the bed.

'No, don't move,' he ordered her when her arms wriggled in the sleeves of the robe, clearly trying to extricate herself. 'Stay exactly as you are.'

He loved the look of her spread out on that sensuous satin quilt, her lower half covered, but her chest and upper arms totally exposed. The paleness of her naked skin against the red silk was incredibly erotic. So was the richness of the red against the pale cream of the bed.

Only one thing was wrong with the picture. Her hair. It should be down.

Her eyes widened when he bent forward to remove the clip that anchored her hair to the top of her head. He heard her breath quicken, watched her eyes follow him as he stroked her hair down over her shoulders, pulling several strands down over her breasts. But not over her nipples.

When he scraped the hair clip over one, her back arched off the bed, her lips falling apart on a startled gasp.

The sight of her stunningly erect nipples reminded him of his own arousal. But he was too intoxicated by her responses now to think about his own frustrations.

He scraped the clip over her other nipple, loving the way her suddenly expanded lungs thrust both her breasts up towards him.

'You like that,' he said throatily, then did it again, and again.

Her answer was a series of soft moans.

Finally, however, the torment became his own, and he threw the clip away, busying his hands on his own body, stripping off his clothes and tossing them aside.

He watched her watch him undress, her eyes telling him that his body met with her approval.

Jason had been blessed with a naturally masculine physique, his shape due more to Mother Nature than with working out. But he did swim every day, and did a hundred situps, both of which keep the flab away and his stomach muscles well toned.

Jason had always felt confident of his body, as well as his lovemaking technique. Usually, he took his time, spending ages on foreplay.

Unfortunately, Leah's eyes staring at him with need sent him right back to where he'd been before he'd started stripping her, desperate to be inside her, driven by a force that was as primal as it was urgent.

Within a flash of being naked, he was with her on the bed, his hands moving with rough caresses over her swollen breasts, his head dipping to take her mouth with a kiss as wild as he was. His lips crushed hers, then drove them apart, his tongue sliding deep, then deeper still.

But it wasn't enough. Not nearly enough. His hand

moved down to pull her robe apart, then her legs, and before his brain could catch up with his body he was between her thighs and pushing into her, groaning as her flesh encased his, its soft slickness enveloping his aching hardness.

Her arms might have been imprisoned by her side, but her legs were free to lift and wrap high around his back. Her bottom lifted with it, the angle of her body taking him in even deeper. It was all a bit much for a man who'd been thinking of nothing else all week but Leah Johannsen.

He slowed his rhythm, trying to last, trying desperately to wait for her. But when she started squeezing him with delicious little movements of her muscles, his body gave up the fight and he came with a raw cry, his body shuddering with the force of his release.

For a split second, his male ego threatened to spoil his ecstasy, but then he heard her cry out his name, and felt her flesh tighten around him like a vice.

His sense of triumph was both physical and emotional. Because he hadn't wanted to be totally selfish. Not tonight. He'd wanted to make it up to her for what that bastard of a husband had done to her. He'd wanted to reassure her that a few scars didn't mar her desirability as a woman.

And it didn't.

Peace came to Jason's body first, leaving him to stare down into her flushed face and watch what his lovemaking had done to her. Her eyes were closed, but her lips were open, panting softly. He felt the last ebbings of her climax. Finally, her legs slipped from around him on a long, voluptuous sigh, and her eyelids fluttered upwards.

He smiled down at her, and she smiled back, her eyes a little embarrassed now, as nice women often were after their first time with a man.

'I'm sorry I was so quick,' he said, bracing his arms on either side of her with his elbows whilst he pushed some strands of hair back from her lovely face.

'You weren't.'

'It's been a while since you've been with a man, hasn't it?'

'Two years.'

'Aah. I see.'

The thought occurred to him that it had only been two weeks since he'd been with Hilary.

Men were different creatures to women. No doubt about that.

He was still tempted to tell her that he'd been thinking of nothing else but her all week, that she was something special to him. But that smacked of an emotional involvement, and he wanted to keep this night strictly physical.

'I'll take longer next time,' he said, deliberately curving his mouth into a wicked smile. 'By the tenth time, you'll be begging me to stop.'

She blinked up at him. 'The *tenth*?'

'Didn't I tell you I was a braggart?'

She laughed. 'No.'

'A braggart and a bastard.'

'I don't believe you.'

'You will, beautiful. You will.'

'Leah...'

Leah surfaced slowly. Dreamily. Happily.

'Mmmm?'

'It's morning,' she heard Jason say through her fog of contentment. 'I have to go.'

Leah opened her eyes to find Jason sitting on the bed beside her, fully dressed in the clothes he'd been wearing when he'd arrived the night before.

'You're going?' she said, still a bit sleep-befuddled. 'But...do you have to rush off? Can't you stay for breakfast at least? It's Saturday, you know.'

'Yes, I know,' he said, his face somewhat grim.

It was then that it came to her what he was saying. He was *going* going.

'I told you last night I wasn't the man for you,' he went on. 'You begged me to stay. So I stayed.'

Leah blinked her surprise. How holier than thou he sounded, as though he'd been forced into staying and accommodating a desperate woman against his better judgement.

'You certainly did,' she agreed, her tone tart.

'I didn't do anything you didn't want me to do, Leah,' he reminded her.

She stared at him, thinking of how she'd given him a lot more than she'd ever given Carl.

There again, he'd given her a lot more than Carl had given her. He'd been incredibly tender and loving that second time. And after that. He certainly wasn't at all grossed out by her scars. He'd even kissed them on one occasion. And washed them in the shower.

The memory of their shower together sent shivers down her spine. She'd washed him too, during which she'd been absolutely shameless. This time together had been as wild as their first with her feet wrapped around his hips.

Then they went back in the bed, for long and languid lovemaking that had ended with her gradually tipping into sleep.

And now here she was, wide awake and being rejected once more.

'You said you had a girlfriend till recently,' she argued, trying to sound calm when inside, desperation was gnawing at her stomach. 'Why can't I be your new girlfriend?'

'You need a man who can love you, Leah. I'm not that man.'

Oh, how it hurt, his saying that he could never love her.

'It…it's not because of the scars, is it?' she heard herself saying in a pitiful voice.

'Don't be ridiculous! Leah, how many times do I have to tell you that your scars don't bother me a bit? Look, if you must know, it's because of my wife, the one you and everyone else thinks I married for her money.

'I didn't,' he growled. 'I loved Karen, more than I could have ever thought possible. Watching her die was terrible. No. *Unbearable.* I thought I would feel relief when she died. Instead, I wanted to die myself.'

'I'm s…sorry,' Leah said, stumbling over the words as she tried to cope with the emotions that his heart-felt confession had produced. Jealousy jabbed at her heart, followed by guilt that she'd judged him so harshly. Finally came the dismaying realisation that the feelings his incredible lovemaking had evoked in her last night would never come to fruition.

Leah knew she could easily fall in love with this man. But what was the point, if he could never love her back?

She was way past being a fool to love. Or she thought she was.

'I'm sorry, too,' he said, and reached out to touch her softly on the cheek.

Tears pricked at her eyes.

'Please don't cry, Leah. Last night was very special. But best we leave it at that.'

'Yes,' she agreed, bravely blinking back the tears.

For a good minute, they maintained an awkward silence, each with their own thoughts.

'Are you still going to resign on Monday?' he asked at last.

'Yes,' she said, nodding. 'Yes, I think that would be for the best.'

'You're right. Of course.'

Leah sighed. It was going to be difficult, living through the two weeks' notice she had to give.

'I'll give you a great reference,' Jason said.

She glared at him for a moment, but then she laughed. 'You'd better.'

He looked at her for a longer moment, and she could have sworn she glimpsed true regret in his eyes.

'I must go,' he said, and stood up abruptly.

She could hardly bear to look at him. Suddenly, she just wanted him to go. Quickly, before she made a right fool of herself.

His bending to kiss her on the forehead made her cringe. She didn't want that kind of kiss from him. She wanted the kind he'd given her last night, the hot hungry intimate kind which had made her squirm and moan. She wanted him to stay. Oh…she just wanted him.

'Just go, for pity's sake!' The words burst from her mouth, sounding bitter and angry.

Leah recalled what he'd said the night before about being a braggart and a bastard. How she wished that he was both! But he wasn't either of them.

She didn't watch him leave. But she heard him shut the front door. It was a horrible sound.

Leah rolled over into her pillows, and wept.

CHAPTER TEN

JOACHIM STRAIGHTENED HIS bow tie, then knocked on Leah's bedroom door.

'It's seven thirty,' he called out. 'The first guests will be arriving soon. I'll wait for you in the foyer.'

'I won't be long,' his daughter replied.

Joachim had barely set foot on the soft blue rug that warmed the cold marble floor of the spacious foyer when the voice of the security man on the gate came through on the intercom, announcing the arrival of a taxi.

'Hope it's not Pollack,' Joachim muttered.

He was just about to dash back up and collect Leah when she started coming down the stairs.

The sight of her literally took his breath away.

She was wearing black. Not a colour he'd ever seen Leah wear before. She always said she didn't like black. But against her fair hair, the black was particularly striking. So was the dress.

It was long, and slinky, and sexy. Yet in a very subtle way, with a deceptively modest top, which was loose fitting and gathered in to a high, round collar. There was a slit, however, which ran from neck to waist at the front, providing the occasional glimpse of cleavage as she moved. Her arms and shoulders were bare as well, Leah's pale skin the perfect foil against the black of the dress.

Her only jewellery was the shoulder-length diamond drop ear-rings, which Joachim had given her for her twenty-second birthday. They'd cost him a small fortune at the time.

'You look simply stunning tonight, Leah,' he complimented when she finally joined him on the rug.

'I'm glad I meet with your approval.'

Joachim heard the edge in her voice and wondered what it meant. Leah had been in an odd mood ever since she'd arrived at the house around three. She confessed she hadn't been to visit the children's wards at Westmead Hospital, as she usually did, claiming she'd woken with a migraine that morning.

Yet she hadn't looked unwell. If anything, she'd looked better than he'd seen her look in ages. If he hadn't known better, he might have thought she'd been lying to him.

But why would she lie? What had she been doing lately that she felt she couldn't admit to?

'Is that dress new?' he asked as he opened the door in anticipation of his first dinner guest—or guests—reaching it. Not Pollack, Joachim saw with relief, but the Hawkinses, long-time friends of the family. Nigel was an orthopaedic surgeon, Jessica his nice but slightly mousy wife. They'd alighted from the taxi, but were still at the bottom of the wide stone steps that led up to the front porch.

'No,' Leah replied. 'Carl bought it for me on our honeymoon. He thought it looked sexy on me.'

Joachim had to agree with his ex son-in-law. His daughter's dress might have worried a father if he was of the narrow-minded, or prudish, kind.

Joachim wasn't. He'd always believed beautiful women like Leah were born to be made love to. And to have children.

But not with any man.

Joachim wanted his next son-in-law to be a man of substance, and character.

He'd had some lingering doubts about Jason Pollack, despite Isabel's voice urging him on, so he'd made a few discreet enquiries on the Monday morning before issuing the dinner invitation, and now felt reassured that Jason Pollack wasn't a fortune hunter, despite the rumours about his first marriage.

His source of information—a journalist friend at a well-known newspaper—gave Pollack a glowing recommendation, both professionally and personally.

Still, if he didn't impress Leah tonight, Joachim resolved to scout around for some other likely candidates to bring into his daughter's life. He wasn't about to let his lovely daughter waste herself, just because her first husband had been less than a man.

'You've done something different with your hair,' he said, noticing when Leah turned away slightly to smooth the long tight skirt over her hips. It was brushed straight back from her face and had been blow-dried dead straight, a shining blonde curtain falling down her back. 'It looks sexy like that.'

She glanced up at him, her glittering green eyes reminding him of Isabel when she was excited about something. 'Do you mind my looking sexy?'

'Not at all. But I thought you didn't want my mystery guest making a pass at you.'

'Is he capable?' she quipped back.

'Any man is capable of a pass. Aah...here's Nigel and Jessie...'

Leah rolled her eyes, then put her mind to playing the role her father wanted her to play for tonight.

Her mother had taught her well how to be a gracious hostess. Leah automatically knew the right things to say to please, plus how to accept a compliment without blushing or stammering.

But she had a moment's worry when Nigel kept staring at her chest. Perhaps she shouldn't have given into the impulse to wear this dress tonight. And to leave off her bra.

But she'd wanted to feel her bare breasts against the silk lining of the dress. Wanted to remember what Jason had done to them last night.

Because that was all she was ever going to have of him. Memories.

Several couples arrived in quick succession, one after the other, all of whom Leah had met before. Her father's stockbroking partners and their wives. His accountant and his wife. His solicitor and his current partner.

A local politician and his second much younger wife made their entrance a few minutes later, soon to be followed by a quite famous television actor with his current live-in lady, along with his agent, a woman Leah's father knew from way back.

Leah guided them all smoothly into the elegant sunken living room, which ran across the back of the house and where a white-coated waiter circled continuously with trays full of pre-dinner drinks. Some couples chose to sit together on the brocade-covered sofas that Leah's mother had been particularly proud of. Others wandered out on to the back terrace to stand by the pool and to admire the view of the harbour, which stretched out before them at the bottom of the garden.

A full moon shone high in the clear night sky, bathing everything in its bright light. The evening was quite warm, which was just as well, Leah thought, given her choice of clothes and lack of underwear.

By eight fifteen, everyone, it seemed, had made an appearance. Everyone except her father's mystery guest. Leah kept mingling as a good hostess should, sipping champagne as she made small talk with her father's friends and colleagues. She was actually enjoying herself more than she'd thought she would. She was even becoming a little curious over their missing guest. Who *was* he? she began to wonder.

Someone who thought himself important enough to be late.

'Maybe your man's stood you up?' Leah murmured somewhat mischievously to her father as she passed by him on her way to the kitchen to check if everything was ready for dinner. Her father might have blind faith in catering companies, but Leah's mother had always said an overseeing eye was necessary for a successful dinner party.

The doorbell rang before she could leave the room.

She turned to glance at her father who smiled, made his excuses and came over to her, taking her elbow and shepherding her back towards the front door.

'Must be our man now,' he said on their way. 'Everyone else is here.'

'He must be seriously rich to have you this eager. But not to worry. I'm ripe and ready for the old coot. Bring him on, I say!'

Her father laughed. 'I'm so glad to see you've finally recovered your sense of humour. But I think you're in for a surprise.'

'Nothing you do would ever surprise me, Daddy,' she replied, lifting her rather tight skirt a little as she mounted the two marble steps that connected the living room with the foyer. 'Mum turned a blind eye to your naughtinesses. And your controlling ways. But I always knew what kind of man you were.'

'Did you now?'

He slanted a smile at her and Leah smiled back. Her father was a bit of a rogue, but a charming and lovable one.

Leah was thinking how much she loved him—despite everything—when he opened the door and there, before her, was the last man she expected to see tonight.

Jason Pollack, dressed in a superb black dinner jacket and looking more devastatingly handsome than she'd ever seen him.

She fairly gaped.

But if she was shocked, so was he.

'Leah!' he blurted out. 'Good God.'

'Leah?' Joachim repeated, staring first at Jason Pollack, then at his daughter. 'You already *know* each other?' he asked her.

'We…er…we met at B…Beville Holdings this week.'

Joachim had never heard his daughter stammer in her life. Or blush the way she was blushing at this moment.

Joachim was no fool. He knew at once that more had gone on between this pair than a simple meeting at work. Intuition told him that Leah's new boss was the reason she had been acted strangely today.

'You never mentioned it,' Joachim said, playing devil's advocate.

'Didn't I?' came her evasive reply.

Joachim became aware that his guest was glowering at both him and her with dark suspicion in his eyes. It occurred to him suddenly that Pollack had no idea Leah was his daughter. Clearly, he'd jumped to the mistaken conclusion that she held a very different but still intimate role in Joachim's life.

That of mistress.

And he looked as jealous as sin.

Joachim felt pleased as punch at this development. But he thought it best to clarify things, post-haste.

'Leah is my daughter, Mr Pollack,' he pronounced proudly, sliding a possessive around her slender waist. 'My only child and the apple of my eye.'

Pollack's deeply set eyes betrayed definite relief, followed by puzzlement. He frowned at Leah, who was still blushing furiously.

'But you go by the name of Johannsen,' he said to Leah, almost accusingly. 'Not Bloom.'

'Her ex-husband's name,' Joachim informed him when Leah couldn't seem to find her tongue. A most unusual occurrence, lately. 'Rich as Croesus, but a cur of a man. Leah is well rid of him, aren't you, sweetheart? But let's not talk of unpleasant things tonight. Dinner will be served shortly. Just enough time for Leah to get you a pre-dinner drink.'

Joachim removed his hand from her waist and leant it lightly on her shoulder, giving her an indulgent smile at the same time. 'I'll leave Mr Pollack in your good hands, shall I, Leah, whilst I check things with the chef.'

Bloom walked off, leaving Jason feeling more rattled than he'd ever felt in his life.

He hadn't been going to come tonight. He hadn't felt like socialising, especially with people he didn't know. It had been Karen's voice in his head saying that it was best not to be alone when you were troubled over something that had driven him out of the house.

So at the last moment he'd thrown on his tux and ordered a taxi, telling himself—as he had earlier in the week—that at least the wine and food would be good.

Seeing Leah standing next to Bloom like that had given him a dreadful shock. For a few stomach-churning moments, he'd entertained appalling thoughts about their relationship. Thank heavens Bloom turned out to be her father, or he didn't know what he might have done.

Jason hadn't realised till that moment just how primal his feelings for Leah had become. One night spent together, and he already thought of her as his, and his alone.

As he stared at her, his mind began stripping her of that far too sexy black dress. He saw her as he'd seen her last night, without a stitch on, her beautiful body stretched out before him, to do with as he pleased.

He'd been trying not to think of her like that all day, telling himself he'd done the right thing to leave things at a one-night stand. But now here she was, tormenting him with her beauty once more.

Still, the pieces of the puzzle that made up Leah Johannsen were finally slotting into place. She was a rich man's daughter. She'd been married to a rich man. Now he understood why she'd had no work record till recently.

'I had no idea you were coming here tonight,' she said agitatedly. 'You have to believe me.'

'I do believe you,' he returned. If she'd expected him, she wouldn't have looked so embarrassed.

'This is all my father's doing,' she said, shaking her head, the action setting those incredible ear-rings swaying and sparkling.

'Yes, I can see that.'

Her eyes flashed with frustration. 'Daddy likes to think he knows what's best for me. He's obviously matchmaking, despite my having told him just last Sunday that I wasn't interested in getting married again. Or falling in love again, for that matter!'

'You're not?' Jason wished she'd told him that this morning.

'No,' she said quite firmly. 'I'm not. Look, the only reason I'm here tonight is because my father asked me to. He said he needed me to sit next to some billionaire he'd invited to dinner and wanted to impress. He refused to tell me your name, though he cleverly let me assume that you were some ageing tycoon whose investment account he wanted to secure. He knew, if I knew your real identity, I wouldn't have agreed to help him.'

'Why not?'

'Because I'm not into wealthy playboy types who think they're God's gift to women,' she threw at him, her delicately pointed chin lifting the way it had that first day in the car park.

Jason opened his mouth to deny he was a playboy. But then closed it again. He supposed he was, in a way. Hilary would certainly describe him as such.

'And please don't throw last night in my face,' she added angrily. 'You caught me at a weak moment. Trust me when I say it won't happen again.'

Jason looked deep into her defiant green eyes, then down at the outline of her stunningly erect nipples before deciding that the lady doth protest too much. Her body language spoke different words to those she was mouthing.

His own body responding to the still-smouldering desire he sensed in hers, Jason wondered how on earth he was going to get through this evening without misbehaving.

'I'm glad you've come over to my way of thinking,' he returned drily. He'd have no hope of containing his own desire if she indicated she'd be willing for a repeat performance. 'Now, how about that drink your father promised?'

CHAPTER ELEVEN

'WHAT A LOVELY room.'

Leah flashed Jason a resentful glance over the rim of her crystal flute. She didn't want to stand here next to him, sipping champagne and pretending that the whole evening was not going to be a total disaster. She didn't want to make small talk with him. She wanted to get out of here more than anything she'd ever wanted, except perhaps this man.

She looked at him hard again and wished he wasn't so attractive. And so decent. If decent was the right word. Maybe he'd just been protecting himself this morning from a girl he decided might become a neurotic cling-on in his life. Clearly, emotional complications weren't on Jason's agenda.

Sex was fine. But nothing more.

Leah wished she could have hidden that she wanted more.

'You can handle this, Leah,' Jason said softly, as if reading her mind. 'You can handle just about anything, from what I've seen. Don't let your father's manipulations bother you. They're irrelevant. I won't be pushed into doing anything I don't want to do. And neither will you. We have minds of our own.'

She stared at him, both impressed and flattered. She really was much weaker than he believed. Around him, anyway.

'And I genuinely like this room,' he added, smiling at her with a warm smile that made her want to weep.

Why couldn't she have married a man like this, instead of Carl? Why couldn't she have met Jason first, before his wife stole his heart and left him without the ability—or the desire—to love again?

'It was my mother's favourite room,' she replied, her heart lurching a little.

'Am I right in presuming that your mother has passed away?'

'She…she died in the same car accident that gave me the scars.'

'I'm so sorry,' he said with true sympathy in his voice and face. 'I never actually knew my mother. She died when I was born. But Dad and I were very close. He passed away when I was in my twenties, so I know what it feels like to lose a much-loved parent.'

'Not a day goes by that I don't miss Mum terribly.'

'I know what you mean,' he muttered. 'You just can't get used to the fact that they're not there any more.'

Leah looked at his bleak eyes and suspected he was now thinking about his wife. Thinking about her and missing her. Every day of his life.

Oh, God.

'Tell me about your mother.'

A wistful sigh whispered from Leah's lips. 'She was a lovely sweet woman, too sweet in some ways. A great wife and mother. She had a wonderfully calming effect in the house, and on Daddy. Everyone loved her. Unfortunately, she was a dreadful driver…'

'Do you look like her, or your father?'

'People say I'm the spitting image of Mum. But not in nature,' she added. 'I'm not quite as amenable as Mum was.'

Jason smiled. 'No kidding.'

Leah felt herself bristle. She opened her mouth to make some snappy reply when her father announced that dinner was ready.

Leah glared at her father as she and Jason walked past on their way into the dining room.

'I want a quiet word with you,' she bit out.

'It won't be during dinner,' came his smiling answer. 'The seating arrangement is not conducive.'

An understatement. The regimented place names put her father at one end of the huge mahogany dining table, and Leah at the other end, almost shouting distance away. Jason had been placed on Leah's immediate right, with Nigel's wife on her left, a shy woman who rarely said a word. No doubt a deliberate ploy on her father's part.

The first two courses were an absolute trial, not because she was forced to talk to Jason and Jason alone, but because he cleverly drew Jessica out of her usual shell till she was fairly sparkling with wit and previously untapped charm.

Jealousy consumed Leah as she watched *all* the women at the table—not just Jessica—flick admiring glances towards Jason. She wanted to scream at them that they couldn't have him. That he was *hers.*

But of course he wasn't.

The trouble was, the memory of his lovemaking was still pleasurably, painfully sharp. She could almost feel his hands on her breasts. Her stomach. Her bottom. Her body literally began to burn as her mind relived that torrid mating in the shower. She could hear her cries echoing against the tiled walls, feel his swollen sex buried deep inside hers.

'Your father's wines are superb.'

'What?' Her head jerked around at his voice, her face flushing when her eyes met his.

Jason was an expert at reading body language. When he'd first started out in sales, his take-home pay had depended on it. There was no doubt in his mind that Leah still wanted him, regardless of what she'd claimed earlier.

His resolve not to sleep with her again shattered under the force of his own immediate and intense desire.

Dessert arrived, a wicked-looking chocolate concoction that had most of the women at the table protesting—though only half-heartedly. Jason used their momentary distraction to lean across the corner of the table towards Leah.

'Come home with me tonight,' he invited softly before he could think better of it.

Her nostrils flared as she sucked in sharply, her eyes blinking wide in shock on him.

'Please,' he added, his own eyes fixed firmly on her stunned face.

Leah just stared at him.

Yes, was the obvious answer. It was what she was wanted more than anything. So why did she hesitate? Why did she feel the urge to punish him for rejecting her this morning?

In that moment, Leah began to understand why pride was one of the seven deadly sins, and not a virtue as some people imagined. It could be perverse, and very self-destructive.

'So what's happened to change your mind?' she snapped, without thinking who might hear.

Fortunately, everyone was busy chatting away to someone else. And also fortunately, Jason didn't take offence. He just smiled at her, as though he'd expected this reaction.

'*You* happened again, Leah,' he said quietly, his eyes gleaming with seductive force. 'Along with that dress. I'm just a man, you know, not a saint.'

'Oh.' His honesty was as irresistibly attractive as he was.

'Is that a yes?'

She nodded, suddenly unable to say a word. Her

mouth had gone as dry as the Sahara. She stared at him again, drowning in his dark, sexy eyes and dying for this dinner to be over so tonight could begin.

The impatience of her desire astounded Leah. Was it just his lovemaking she was craving? Or the man himself?

Impossible to separate them. The man *and* his lovemaking. They came together, as they had come together, last night, not once but several times.

This had to be why Trish had kept going back to Jim, even though she knew there was no future with him. Because the sex was great.

Leah couldn't imagine anything, however, being as perfect or as powerful as what she'd shared with Jason last night. How was she going to feel when he called it quits a second time?

And he would. If not tomorrow morning, then eventually.

Don't think about that, she told herself as she dropped her eyes to the dessert and picked up her spoon.

Leah was partial to chocolate of any kind. But her taste buds seemed to have gone on strike, her focus on nothing but what was going to happen later tonight after she went home with Jason.

Slowly, she lifted her head and gazed down the long table to where her father was enthusiastically attacking his dessert. Perhaps feeling her eyes on him, he stopped with his dessert fork mid-air and looked back across the expanse of mahogany.

The smile that curved her lips was full of irony. Whatever her father had planned for tonight, it certainly wasn't for his daughter to go home with his mystery guest.

Clearly, her father was on the lookout for a new son-in-law, not a new client.

Joachim Bloom believed in love and marriage and family. Even before Leah married the first time, he'd expressed the wish for a grandson, his one regret over his own marriage being that they hadn't been able to have more children.

Leah would have liked to give her father what he wanted. *This* time. Unfortunately, the man sitting beside her was never going to marry her, or fall in love with her. He certainly didn't want her having his child. He'd made his position quite clear, both this morning and tonight. His offer of another night together was a strictly sexual one.

Leah knew her only chance of having any kind of relationship with Jason, as opposed to just one more night, lay in her ability to convince him that this was all she wanted, too.

Could she do that? Would he believe her?

It was a plus that she'd already revealed tonight that she didn't want to get married again. All she had to do was slip in somewhere that she didn't want to fall in love again, either.

A shudder ran through Leah. She'd never been all that good a liar.

'You don't like chocolate?' Jason enquired.

Leah hardly dared look at him, lest he see the machinations going on in her mind. 'I seem to have lost my appetite.'

'Just as long as you're not dieting.'

'I'm not. When I'm upset or excited, I simply can't eat.'

'And are you upset over something?' he asked softly, the implication behind his clever question drawing her eyes to his.

'No.'

'When I'm upset or excited, I eat all the more,' he said, his dessert already gone.

'And are you upset over something?' she heard herself ask on a husky whisper.

'No,' he mouthed in reply.

Leah swallowed. How on earth was she going to bear the rest of the evening? But her father's dinner parties were never rushed affairs.

After dessert, coffee and cognac would be served back in the living room, along with large cheese and fruit platters. Finally, bottles of his prized port would come out. No one would be expected to leave till midnight, at least. No one ever left Joachim Bloom's dinner parties early. No one ever wanted to. Except when they were desperate to be dragged by their sexy new boss into bed and kept there.

By the time everyone rose from the dining table, Leah began thinking about places she could take Jason to where she could at least be alone with him, where they could talk naturally and not in hushed whispers or coded messages, where he might kiss her and touch her and maybe even…

'I'm taking Jason down to the boathouse to look at your cruiser, Daddy,' she said to her father as soon as the time came to leave the table. 'He's interested in buying a boat. You did say you wanted to sell it, didn't you?'

'But only if it's a bargain,' Jason piped up by her side, not batting an eyelid at this invention of Leah's. What a clever man he was. What a gorgeous, clever, co-operative man!

Leah's father gave a mock sigh. 'I see I'll have to teach my daughter the art of negotiation. Never show your hand, Leah. Make people think you don't want to give them what they want. That the way, isn't it, Jason?'

'Most of the time,' Jason replied with a brilliant poker face. 'There are occasions, however, when it is more…effective…to let a person know what you want. Don't you agree?'

'Indeed I do,' her father said, glancing from Jason to Leah and smiling a rather smug smile. 'Off you go then, Leah, and show this young man my boat. But leave the final negotiation of any sale to me.'

Jason took her hand the moment they were alone on the terrace, pulling her off to one side into the shadows and pressing her up against a side wall.

'This is what you want, isn't it?' he muttered just before his mouth collided with hers.

The kiss was long and wet and wild, leaving Leah's lips bruised and her heart thundering in her chest. Who knew what she would have allowed then and there if he hadn't taken her hand again and started pulling her past the pool towards the garden beyond.

She didn't say a word during their silent journey down the moonlit pathway that led to the boathouse. What was there to be said even if she was capable of saying it?

'Is it locked?' Jason threw at her when they neared the boathouse.

'Yes. But I know where the key is.'

'I'm sure you do.'

He sounded angry, she realised. Either that or just as impatient as she was.

'You're not angry with me, are you?' she asked when they reached the boathouse door.

He swung her round, then yanked her hard against him.

'Angry with myself, more like it,' he ground out, and kissed her again, this time for even longer. By the time his head lifted, she'd forgotten the thread of their conversation.

'The key,' he demanded. 'Where's the damned key?'

Her hands were shaking as she reached round behind a nearby downpipe and removing a small black magnetised box, sliding it open and retrieving the key.

Jason took it from her and jammed it into the lock. The hinges creaked a little as he pushed open the door.

'Is there a light in here somewhere?'

'Do we have it turn it on?'

'We do, if I'm to look at this boat.'

'You mean you actually do want to look at the boat?'

'Only the part where the bunks are.'

'Oh.'

She turned on the light.

The boathouse was just large enough to house her father's cruiser, a sleek white vessel, which did have sleeping quarters below deck. The sight of her mother's name painted on the side, however, had a dampening effect on Leah's passion. So did the musty smell inside the boathouse. When she heard something rodent-like scurrying beneath some empty cartons piled up in a corner, she squealed and grabbed Jason's arm.

'What's wrong?'

'I...I think I heard a mouse. Or maybe a rat.'

'A rat...'

'Yes. I hate rats,' she said, and shuddered.

Jason almost told her that she was mistaken. She liked rats. She'd married one, hadn't she? And she was about to have an affair with another one.

After all, nothing had changed since this morning. He still couldn't offer her anything more than his body.

Unfortunately, the state of Jason's body refused to totally let him change his mind about taking her again. But he could wait a little longer. He didn't have to do it here, in a wretched boathouse.

'Let's go,' he said, grabbing her hand and dragging her back outside into the moonlight.

'Go where?'

He locked the door and put the key back in its box.

'I'm taking you home to my nicely air-conditioned and rodent-free apartment.'

'Right now, you mean?'

'Yes.'

'But the dinner party isn't over.'

'It is for us.'

CHAPTER TWELVE

'HOW ON EARTH did you manage that?' Leah asked as the taxi sped from Vaucluse to the city.

Jason curved an arm around her shoulders and pulled her close. 'Manage what?'

'Manage to get me out of there in double-quick time with my father's approval.'

'Simple. While you were in the powder room, I told him the truth.'

'You *told* him I'd be spending the night with you?'

'Not in so many words. I said I was taking you on to a nightclub. Your father's an intelligent man. He doesn't have to have everything spelled out for him.'

'But you don't understand. I wasn't going back to my place after the dinner party. I was going to stay the night at home. I usually do every Saturday night. My father will expect to see me at breakfast.'

'You'll have to give him a call tomorrow morning then, won't you? Tell him you didn't come home and won't be down for breakfast.'

Leah groaned.

'Leah, darling.' Jason's voice was firm. 'You're a beautiful, twenty-six-year-old divorcée living in Sydney in the twenty-first century. Your father realises you have a sex life.'

'But I haven't,' she denied. 'I mean…last night was the first time since…since…'

'Yes. I know that. But that was only because you were self-conscious about your scars. You're over that nonsense now, aren't you?'

'Am I?'

'Absolutely.' And, as if to prove it, he slid his hand up under her dress and caressed the ridges which criss-crossed her left thigh.

Leah's first reaction was to stiffen, but, gradually, she melted under his gentle touch, her breath quickening when his fingers moved further up her thigh to press against the already damp satin of her black G-string.

The contact of his fingertips against electrified nerve-endings twisted her stomach into knots, her belly tightening as the tension began to build down there. If he kept doing what he was doing, she would come, right there, in the back of the taxi.

Her eyes darted to the back of the driver's head, then at the tall buildings flying past. She sucked in sharply and tried to think of other things.

'See?' he murmured into her right ear. 'You're cured. And we're here.'

The taxi lurching to a halt at the curb coincided with his hand abandoning her.

A low moan of frustration escaped her lips before she could stop it. She looked at him with desperate eyes, and he dropped a light kiss on her mouth.

'Not much longer to wait,' he murmured before climbing out of the taxi first. Once on the pavement, he turned to help her out on to her feet, then paid the driver through the front window.

Unfortunately, to do so, he had to let go of her hands.

How did she manage to stand up all by herself? Her bones had gone to water and her head was spinning out into the stratosphere.

By the time the taxi sped off, Leah was teetering on her high heels. Jason caught her against him as she swayed.

'You drank far too much wine over dinner,' he said, holding her tightly against him as he ushered her into the tower like building.

Had she? She couldn't remember. Dinner had become a bit of a blur.

The security guards behind the reception desk waved to Jason on his way past, but he just nodded to them, then steered her into one of the empty lifts in the far corner of the massive foyer and inserted his key card.

'You're not going to fall asleep on me, are you?' he asked a bit worriedly during the lift ride upwards.

'I certainly hope not.'

He smiled. 'That's my girl.'

She stared up at him and thought how much she'd like to be his girl.

'And what does that look mean?' he chided, tipping her chin up with his fingertips.

'Nothing. Please kiss me.'

'Yes, ma'am.'

Jason was happy to do just that, happy to take her mouth and let desire obliterate the qualms that kept surfacing whenever he was with this girl. Soon, he wasn't thinking of anything much except the need to have her in his arms once more.

The lift slid to a smooth halt on the top floor of the tower, the doors opening straight into his luxury penthouse apartment.

But neither of them had eyes for anything but each other. Jason couldn't wait any longer, swinging her around against the wall and pinning her there with his body. His hands clasped her head and his kisses turned savage.

The need for air finally forced him to wrench his mouth away. But there would be no slowing down. No waiting this time.

He didn't undress her, or himself. He just yanked open his zipper and lifted her dress. Her panties gave way with a ripping sound and then he was there, wedging himself between her legs and pushing up into her deliciously ready body.

Once safely anchored, he straightened, then let the dress fall, his hands lifting to cup her face.

'I don't want to hurt you,' he said thickly, aware that his rough penetration had stretched her up on to her toes.

'You're not.'

'But I might,' he said with a grimace. His passion for her had been uncontrollable from the start, appealing to his dark side, making him forget all common sense and decency.

'No, no.' She shook her head violently against his hands. 'I'm fine. Please. Just do it, Jason.'

Her urgency stirred his dark side ever further. As Jason began to pump up into her, he vowed to make her want him like this all the time. He would keep her here with him for the rest of the weekend, making love to her over and over till having him inside her was as natural to her as breathing. He'd make her crave sex as she had never craved it before. And with the craving would come complete surrender to his will.

By Monday morning, there would be no more talk of resigning. She would be totally at his beck and call, both at work and here, every single night. She'd be his, in every way. Unable to say no. Every man's fantasy come true.

'Mine,' he muttered against her mouth when she splintered apart. His own climax swiftly followed, Jason hoisting her up on to his hips whilst his flesh was still pulsing inside of hers.

Her forehead flopped against his shoulder, her arms winding up around his neck. A sigh of satisfaction whispered at the base of his throat.

'That was incredible,' she murmured as he carried down towards the master bedroom. 'You're incredible.'

Leah felt his arms stiffen around her. His step even

faltered for a moment. She knew she'd have to say something very quickly to redress the damage she'd just done. If not, tonight would become just another one-night stand.

'You're a much better lover than Carl, you know,' she went on hurriedly, lifting her head to throw what she hoped was a saucy smile up at him.

He laughed, which was good. 'So good sex matters to you?'

'I was one of those romantically foolish females who imagined true love did the trick for them. And then you came along and proved me wrong.'

His smile had an odd edge to it. 'We aim to please.'

'I wish I'd met someone like you sooner.'

Now he ground to a total halt. 'What do you mean by that?'

Her shrug was magnificently nonchalant. 'You know. Someone whose only priority is having a good time, and has the know-how to deliver it. We're perfect for each other, Jason. You don't want love and marriage, and neither do I. I've been there, done that, and I'm not in a hurry to go there again.'

Leah could not tell if he believed her, or not.

'Which reminds me,' she raced on. 'You're going to have to start using condoms soon. This weekend should be safe, but, in a day or two, we'll be entering danger territory.'

The horror on his face underlined how much Jason didn't want consequences. Or commitment. Or complications.

'I'd forgotten all about that! Damn, but you do make me lose it, Leah.'

Her smile carried some degree of satisfaction. 'Do I?'

'You know you do. I can't seem to get enough of you.'

'Mmm. Yes. I'm beginning to feel the evidence of that for myself,' she purred. 'So what do you want to do about it?'

'First things first. As much I like this dress on you, I prefer you without it. And those earrings will have to go. I might end up swallowing one and be charged with grand larceny. Then we're going to share a spa bath.'

'And after that?'

His dark eyes glittered. 'Don't you worry your pretty little head about the wheres and wherefores of tonight,' he said as he carried her into a bedroom that looked like a photo spread in a glossy magazine for what a bachelor's bedroom should be like. 'I like to be the boss in the bedroom as well as at work.'

Leah could see that already. But she didn't mind. She found his take-charge attitude exciting. Carl had never made love to her anywhere but in bed.

Leah realised now that her husband had been a lazy lover. And lacking in passion.

There again, he'd never really loved her, had he? She'd meant little more to him that one of the multi-million-dollar paintings he bought and displayed so proudly to everyone. She'd been a prized possession to show off. A status symbol. Joachim Bloom's daughter.

Jason didn't care that she was Joachim Bloom's daughter. He'd wanted her when he thought she was just a working girl.

They stood in the middle of the room. Their bodies were pressed tightly together. Leah wriggled her hips against Jason, making him gasp.

'Do it to me again, Jason,' she said, hardly recognising the husky voice that came out of her mouth. 'On that big bad bed of yours. The bath can wait. I can't.'

He laughed. '*I'm* the one supposed to be doing the seducing around here.'

'Then hurry up and seduce me again.'

'I thought I told you I like to be the boss.'

'I forgot.'

'I'll forgive you this once,' he said as he laid her carefully back across the black-and-white jungle print spread. Leah gasped with surprise when he pushed her long tight skirt upwards till it enveloped her upper half—and her head—in darkness.

Leah had never known anything so erotic. She could not see him. But she could feel him, as he pushed into her and then slid in and out, filling her, then leaving her feeling momentarily frustrated as he pulled back. His stroke was slow and strong, teasing her, pleasing her. That delicious tension began to build again, catching at her breath, making her muscles tighten around him.

She bit her bottom lip when he took hold of her hips and picked up his rhythm. She could hear him now as well as feel him. His breath was ragged, his fingertips quite brutal as they dug into her flesh. She'd be bruised in the morning, but she didn't care.

He was like some wild beast, holding her hard against him while he shuddered into her.

And then he was gone, leaving her lying there, with her dress still up over her face, her arms up-stretched, her legs apart, her body spent.

She heard water running, but still could not move. Finally, he came back to her and with gentle hands removed her dress. Not just from her face, but from her whole body.

She looked up to see that he was naked, too. Naked and smiling. When he stretched out beside her and started playing with her breasts, Leah realised that she wasn't as spent as she thought she was.

'I'm running us that spa bath,' he murmured, deserting her nipples to remove her ear-rings. 'Do you want to give your father a call tonight?' he asked as he dropped them one by one on his glass-topped bedside table. 'You could warn him you won't be back.'

'No, I…I don't think so. I'll call him in the morning.'

'He won't be worried, you know. This is what you said he wanted. You and me together.'

'I still can't believe you were his mystery guest. But he read some article about you in last Sunday's paper. It seemed to impress him. He showed it to me.'

'It didn't impress *you* though, did it? You weren't at all impressed when we met on Monday.'

'You've impressed me now that I've gotten to know you. Biblically speaking, that is.'

His hand went back to her breast, his expression speculative as he played with her nipple some more. 'Is this all you want me from me, Leah?' he asked when she gave a small moan of pleasure. 'You won't start wanting more, will you?'

Leah's heart twisted. She ached to throw at him that of course she would. She already did. But sex was all he was offering. So she said, 'That, and companionship. I've been very lonely since my divorce. I'm sure you can manage to deliver both, can't you?'

'No trouble. But I'll have to go condom shopping tomorrow. I do have a couple in my wallet, which I put there for emergencies. And possibly one or two in the bathroom somewhere. But with you, beautiful,' he said, tweaking her nipple again. 'I'm going to need some serious restocking.'

'I'll take that as a compliment,' she said with what she hoped was a sexy smile.

Leah knew full well that she was risking heartbreak by having an affair with Jason. But to give him up was out of the question. She simply could not resist the wild abandon that he evoked in her, and the sexual pleasure he gave her.

Already she was looking forward to that bath, to washing him all over, and being washed in return.

'You'd better check that bath,' she said. 'We don't want a flood.'

'Let's check it together,' he suggested, and scooped her up into his arms.

CHAPTER THIRTEEN

LEAH WOKE FIRST the next morning, surprised to find how natural it felt to lie next to Jason. She just rested there beside him for a minute or two, looking around the spacious bedroom and thinking how little she actually liked his apartment.

She'd seen enough of it last night to form an opinion.

It was huge, of course. Huge and modern, with lots of glass and black leather, along with acres of white tiles, stainless steel appliances and geometrically patterned rugs. The walls were all white, the artwork mostly black and white, the lighting recessed. There were no curtains anywhere, just darkly tinted windows and sliding glass doors, leading out on to grey stone terraces.

The interior decorator, whoever he or she was, obviously had no liking for colour. The place was cold and soulless.

Leah hated it.

But she loved the man who lived here.

Her eyes slid over to where he was still sprawled out on the other side of the massive bed, a black satin sheet tangled around the lower half of his magnificent body.

Leah liked the opportunity to look at his sleeping face, to trace his features with admiring eyes and try to work out what made him so attractive to her.

She could find no fault in his face. Everything was perfect. His high, wide forehead. His straight, but symmetrical eyebrows. His elegantly shaped nose. His squared chin. His lovely mouth.

Oh, yes, his mouth most of all, with its strongly sculptured upper lip and sexily full bottom lip. The perfect combination of masculinity and sensuality.

Leah didn't like to think it was just his handsomeness that drew her. But maybe it was. Because she'd been right when she'd told him last night that she only knew him biblically.

What did she really know about him other than what she'd read in that paper, plus the little he'd told her?

A lot more, her love for him piped up. You know a lot more!

Jason was a man quickly liked and respected by his employees. A man who hated taking advantage of a vulnerable woman. A man who was honest about what he wanted and didn't want.

And he was a man who'd once loved too much.

Leah had seen the pain in his eyes when he'd talked about his wife. She recognised that type of pain. She'd seen it in the mirror in her own eyes after her mother died. Then to a lesser degree, after Carl left her.

Loss could be a terrible thing when you cared. And Jason had cared.

Caring in a man was a good thing. It showed depth, and character.

Feeling better about loving him, Leah rose and tiptoed to the bathroom where she set about inspecting the damage in the vanity mirror.

There were faint fingerprint bruises on her hips and on her breasts. And one deeply purple love bite on her neck.

Leah touched it, surprised that it didn't hurt too much, but infinitely grateful that she had long hair, which could cover the evidence of her night of wild sex.

Not that she would bother to cover any of the bruises whilst she was here, in Jason's place. She rather liked the thought of his seeing what he'd done to her last night. Liked the thought of parading herself naked for him again today as well.

He'd insisted on her staying nude last night, not letting her cover up with a robe, forcing her to finally get over her squeamishness about her scars. After a while, she'd become quite shameless, and not at all self-conscious.

Pushing her hair back from her shoulders, she returned to the bedroom, and glanced back over at the bed.

Jason was still asleep.

The stainless steel digital clock on his glass-topped bedside table said it was ten past nine. Mrs B. was unlikely to have looked in her room as yet and discover she hadn't come home the night before. She would presume Leah was sleeping in late after the dinner party.

Leah would ring her father this morning, but a little later on.

Leah still felt irritated with him for doing what he'd done last night, inviting Jason to dinner, then letting her think his mystery guest was some rich old codger. He really should not interfere in other people's lives. He should be taught a lesson.

It would serve him right if she announced over the telephone this morning that she'd become Jason Pollack's mistress. Which was virtually what she now was.

Some time during the night, Jason had asked her not to resign, and to move into the penthouse with him. She'd refused on both counts. To work with him every day and sleep with him every night would be courting disaster. She'd survived Carl leaving her. She would not survive Jason leaving her.

At the same time she could not resist him totally. So she told him he could stay the night at her place when he wanted to, and vice versa. But she would not wrap her life solely around him. She would find herself another job and keep her own place. Because she knew that one day—and this was the part she didn't say to him—one day, he would grow tired of her as he had his previous girlfriend, and she would be cast adrift from his life.

The thought was horrible enough at it was. How much worse would the eventuality be if she worked and lived with the man, twenty-four seven?

Leah sighed, then wandered across to the wide, plate-glass window that faced east and was currently drenched in morning sunshine. She moved to press herself against the glass, soaking in its warmth, her arms lifting up in a languid stretch, flattening her breasts and tightening her belly.

It was a highly erotic stance. Not something she would ever have done before meeting Jason. But she revelled in it this morning, well aware that last night had changed her for ever. She was now a different creature. Much more sexually driven, her senses heightened, her desires expanded.

Common sense kept warning her against becoming too involved with a man who was never going to give what she now wanted: to be his wife and the mother of his children.

Common sense, however, didn't feel like this. It didn't send delicious shivers down her spine. Or make her body yearn and burn in a thousand exciting ways.

Neither did common sense ever make her forget, even for a moment, that she was basically still alone. During Jason's lovemaking she could pretend that everything was all right.

Even though it wasn't…

'My God, you're *her*!'

Leah whirled to the sound of Jason's voice, blinking madly to rid herself of the tears that had welled up in her eyes.

Jason was sitting up in bed, his expression both startled and excited. The black sheet was still over his lower half, for which she was grateful.

'Her who?' she asked, walking quickly back towards the bed. Some embarrassment had resurfaced at being discovered standing there like that.

'The girl in my dream.'

'What girl in what dream?' she asked as she dived under the sheet and pulled it up over her breasts.

'The dream I had just before I bought Beville Holdings. About this girl on a billboard advertising their shampoo. She was photographed from the rear, naked, with lovely long fair streaming down her bare back. She looked exactly like you looked a second ago…'

When he reached over to run his hands down her long fall of hair, his amazed expression abruptly changed to a frown. 'Good Lord, look at the state of your neck! Did I do that?'

'Do you see anyone else in this bed with me?'

'Why didn't you stop me?'

Leah laughed. 'Why don't I turn back the tides as well?'

'I can't believe I did that,' he murmured, his eyes back to amazed, his fingertips tracing the love bite.

'There's a few marks on my breasts and hips as well. But nothing quite like this one.'

'Will makeup hide them?' he asked unexpectedly.

'Possibly. But I'm not exactly going to walk round naked, except when I'm with you.'

'That depends.'

'Depends on what?'

'On whether I can talk you into becoming the face of Beville Holdings products.'

'What?'

'I've outlined a new advertising campaign based on that dream I had. I spoke to Harry about it yesterday and he said that its success would depend on my getting the right model.'

'Harry who?'

'Harry Wilde. He's an advertising genius and a friend of mine.'

'But I'm no model, Jason.'

'You're more beautiful than most.'

'But…but what about my scars?'

'No one will see them. I promise.'

'The photographer will.'

'You don't have to be really naked. You just have to look like you're naked from the back from the hips up. You can wear a low-slung sarong. And stick things over your breasts.'

'I don't know, Jason…'

'You'd be perfect, Leah. And you'd enjoy it.'

'I doubt it.'

'The pay would be good as well. Better than your current salary.'

'I don't really need my salary, Jason. I have this trust fund from my mother and—'

'Leah, you *like* earning your own money,' he broke in. 'Otherwise, why did you go and get a job in the first place?'

'I wanted to prove to myself that I could do it.'

'Which you have done. And I applaud you for it. Now give yourself a new challenge and do this.'

'You're very persuasive, aren't you?'

'That's what I've been trained to be.'

'You're far too used to getting your own way.'

'I haven't with you. You won't even move in with me.'

'You'll survive.'

'You loved him a lot, didn't you?'

The question threw Leah for a second. 'You don't usually marry someone you don't love,' came her careful reply.

'True.'

'This conversation has turned far too serious for me,' Leah said. 'I'm going to have a shower, then go into that dental-white kitchen of yours and make breakfast.'

'You don't like this place much, do you?' he said before she could escape the bed. 'Go on. Tell me the truth.'

'The truth? Okay. I think it's the coldest, most soulless apartment I've ever been in.'

He laughed a delighted laugh. 'I do, too.'

'Then why did you buy it?'

'Because it was convenient and a good investment. And because it matched its owner at the time,' he added, but without that haunted look she'd seen in his face before.

'Decisions made after someone dies are never good ones,' she told him. 'My father was going to sell the family home after Mum died. I dare say he might have bought something like this. He's all for good investments. I fought him tooth and nail and he didn't sell in the end. But I'm still a bit worried. It's not a good sign that he wants to sell the boat he named after Mum.'

'I could buy the boat for you, if you like.'

Leah glowered at him. 'You are not to buy me anything, Jason Pollack. Nothing expensive, anyway. Flowers and chocolates are fine. But no boats, or diamonds, or any of the other tell-tale gifts that rich men buy their beck-and-call girls.'

'You're not my beck-and-call girl,' he growled, pulling her over on top of him. 'Though I'd like you to be.'

'Would you just?'

'Damn right, I would,' he muttered, pushing her up into a sitting position, her knees on either side of his hips.

'I said I was going to have a shower,' she told him, trying not to give in to the urges he spurred in her. 'I have to ring home as well. As much as I'm still peeved with my father, I don't want to worry him.'

'Afterwards.'

'I...I'm not really in the mood for more sex right now, Jason.'

'Liar. I can *see* that you're lying. You can watch *me* come, if you'd prefer.'

Leah's head spun with his words. The idea excited her. She'd never done that. She'd always been too caught up in the act herself. How would it feel to remain fully in control whilst he lost it?

Taking a deeply gathering breath, Leah lifted herself up on to her knees, then reached down to take him in her hand, rubbing him till a tortured moan slipped from his mouth. Finally, she put him just inside her, then sank slowly downwards.

'You do realise,' she said when their bodies were together, 'that I'm not the only girl at Beville Holdings sleeping with her boss.'

Conversation, Leah hoped, would distract her from her own rapidly escalating excitement. Maybe she'd be able stay more detached if she chatted away to him.

'Hell, Leah, I'm not interested in talking about Trish and Jim right now.'

'I wasn't talking about Trish and Jim. I meant Shelley and Jim.'

His eyebrows lifted. 'So what else do you know that I don't know?'

'Management have wasted a lot of money lately.'

'You think I should sack the lot?'

'I think you should offer them incentives to leave.'

He smiled. 'You'd make me a good Girl Friday, you know. Say the word and I'll promote you.'

'I think you should settle for me being the face of Beville Holdings. I don't like the idea of sleeping with the boss.'

'I'll still be your boss.'

'No, you won't. As of next week, I'm signing myself up with a proper modelling agency. You'll have go through them if you want me.'

'I want you,' he said, his dark eyes gleaming as he grabbed her hips and began moving her up and down.

Yes, he did, Leah conceded with a rush of hot blood through her body. For now.

But not for ever.

'Lean forward,' he ordered her. 'Stretch your arms up over my head.'

'No. I'm supposed to be staying all cool while I just watch you.'

'Just do it, Leah.'

She did it, the position setting her breasts swinging towards his face, and his mouth. He licked the aching tips, then took one between his teeth.

The pain was delicious, but swiftly unbearable. She wrenched her breast out of his mouth, and straightened.

'You have to stop doing things like that,' she told him breathlessly.

'Why?'

'Because I might get to like it.'

'I hope so.'

'You have a wicked side to you, Jason Pollack.'

He laughed. 'And don't you just love it.'

She blushed. Not her first blush since she'd climbed into that taxi with him last night.

'And I love that about you, too,' he murmured, reaching up to stroke her pink cheeks before running his fingertips down over her breasts, down her taut belly into the damp golden curls that surrounded her sex. 'You haven't been like this with any other man, not even your precious Carl. *Have* you?' he demanded as he touched her there, where her nerve endings were gathered into an apex of exquisite sensitively.

'No,' she confessed shakily.

'Only with me,' he rasped. 'You *are* my beck-and-call girl, Leah. Make no mistake about that. But only because you want to be,' he said as his hand withdrew to take hold of her hips once more. 'You do want to be, don't you?' he said as he urged her on.

She didn't answer him. Just closed her eyes…

CHAPTER FOURTEEN

JOACHIM BLOOM HAD just finished breakfast when the phone rang. He guessed who it was before he answered it.

'It's me, Daddy,' Leah said with a touch of defiance in her voice.

'So I see,' he replied calmly. 'Am I to presume you stayed the night at Pollack's place?'

'Jason, Daddy. Call him Jason. And, yes, that's where I stayed. Did…er…Mrs B. say anything this morning when I didn't make it down for breakfast?'

'No. I told her you went out to a nightclub with a gentlemen friend late last night and wouldn't be back till later today.'

'That was presumptuous of you. What did she say?'

'I'm not quite sure. She mumbles a bit, does Mrs B. But it sounded something like, *it's about time*.'

'Oh…'

Joachim smiled. 'You sound piqued that we're not all shocked out of our skins, Leah.'

'I'm not shocked *you're* not shocked. After all, you

threw us together on purpose, didn't you? Though Lord knows why. That's what I'd like to know, Daddy. Why pick a man for me like Jason Pollack?'

Joachim knew it would sound ridiculous if he said, 'Your mother suggested him to me.'

'I liked the look of him in the paper,' he said instead. 'I like self-made men.'

'You implied to me that he'd married his first wife for his money.'

'Did I? I don't recall doing that. Maybe that was you, jumping to that conclusion. So, what do you think now that you know him better? Did he marry his first wife for her money?'

'No. He married her because he loved her. So much so that he never wants to fall in love again, or get married again.'

Joachim's dismay was sharp. It seemed he'd made a big mistake here.

Serve him right for listening to so-called messages from the afterlife. He'd never believed in the supernatural before. He suddenly felt very foolish for following that voice in his head. Of course it hadn't been Isabel talking to him, he reprimanded himself sternly. How could he ever have imagined it?

'I'm sorry, Leah. Are you very angry with me?'

'Not angry, Daddy. Just a bit annoyed. You really should learn to butt out of other people's lives. If and when I want another husband, *I* will find him. Do I make myself clear?'

'Absolutely.'

'Meanwhile, Jason and I do like each other. A lot. So don't be shocked if the tabloids start calling us an item. I suspect we're going to be seen out and about a bit together in the coming weeks. Oh, and another thing. I'm resigning my job at Beville Holdings on Monday and becoming a model.'

'A *model*! But…but…'

'Yes, I know. My scars. Obviously, I won't be becoming a swimwear model. But not to worry. I have my first contract in the bag. I'm to be the face of Beville Holdings products in a new advertising campaign they're launching in a few months.'

'You're joking.'

'Not at all. There has to some benefit to being the boss's mistress.'

'Mistress!'

'Mistress. Girlfriend. Whatever.'

Joachim finally heard it in his daughter's voice. The underlying pain. There could only be one reason for it. She'd fallen in love with Jason Pollack.

For a split second, Joachim felt devastated. Till that damned voice piped up in his head again, whispering that everything would be all right.

Against all logic, relief flooded his soul.

Have faith, my darling, the voice whispered to him.

It *was* Isabel's voice. He recognised it.

Joachim had to clear his throat to speak. 'That's good,' he said. 'Jason's a good man.'

'Daddy, have you been drinking?'

'Only coffee.'

'He just wants me for the sex. You do realise that, don't you?'

'Lots of relationships begin with just sex, daughter,' Joachim pointed out reasonably.

'He's still in love with his wife!'

'Possibly, he is. Love doesn't die just because of death. But she is dead, Leah, and you're very much alive. So is Jason.'

'Jason knows what he wants and doesn't want, Daddy. He's been very honest with me. Right from the start.'

'And when was the start, daughter?'

Leah sighed a weary sounding sigh. 'Friday night. After work.'

'I see.' Joachim didn't really see.

Have faith, Joachim.

'Just love him, Leah. There's no man on earth who could resist a girl like you loving him.'

'Oh, Daddy,' she suddenly sobbed on the other end of the line. 'I do so love him. It's nothing like I felt for Carl. I…I…'

'There, there, child,' he soothed. 'Everything will be fine. You'll see.'

'No, it won't,' she cried, then sniffed. 'I have to go. Jason will be out of the bathroom soon. I probably won't be back today. I'll call you later in the week,' she said, and hung up.

Leah lay face-down on the bed whilst she listened to the shower running and Jason whistling. He was happy and she was crying.

That was because he was getting what he wanted and she never would.

The time to get out of this relationship is now, Leah. Not in a few weeks, or a few months. Now, before it goes any further.

But she knew she didn't have the courage to do that. How could she possibly say, 'Sorry, Jason,' when he came out of that bathroom, 'but I've fallen in love with you and you're never going to love me back, so I've decided to call it a day.'

Impossible.

No, she'd smile and go along with what he wanted today. And every other day till he called it quits. That was her destiny now.

No, that's your *choice*, her brain reminded her.

Maybe. But does love ever really have a choice? And if it does, is that choice ever going to be the right one?

The bathroom door opened, and a dripping wet Jason emerged in a cloud of steam, a white towel slung low around his hips.

'I've been thinking,' he said, one hand lifting to fingercomb his hair back from his forehead.

'Yes?' Leah propped her chin up on her hands and did her best to look nonchalant.

'About your resigning…'

'What about my resigning,' she repeated warily. She hoped he wasn't going to try to talk her out of that again!

'I think it's a good idea. I could never keep my mind on the job with you around. I'd be wanting to find excuses to get you alone all the time. But you'll have to show up tomorrow. It'll take Bob a day or two to line up a temp.'

'Mandy could do the job. She fills in for me occasionally.'

'Are you sure?'

'Quite sure.'

'Best you still come in tomorrow.' He spun round and was about to walk back into the bathroom when he stopped and turned back again. 'Did you ring your father?'

'Yes.'

'I'll bet he wasn't at all shocked.'

'You're quite right, Jason,' she returned coolly. 'He wasn't.'

'See? You were worried for nothing.'

'I told him about my two new jobs.'

'*Two* new jobs?'

'Yes. Model and mistress.'

'For pity's sake, Leah.' Jason scowled. 'You are not my mistress. You'll have your father thinking I'm a worse cad than that creep you were married to. You're my girlfriend.'

'One in a long line.'

'That's not true,' he denied, his expression serious. 'Okay, so I had a lot of girlfriends in my younger days. But you are only the second girlfriend I've had since my wife died.'

And the first one I've really cared about, Jason could have added. But didn't.

Leah sat up abruptly. 'You're kidding me.'

'Not at all. I didn't date for four years after Karen's death. I just didn't want to. But about six months ago I met someone at a party, and I realised my celibate days were over.'

'And that was the girlfriend you broke up with recently?'

'Yes, Hilary. She was a nice enough woman, but she wanted marriage. I'd told her right from the start that I wouldn't marry again, so I felt I had no choice but to break it off. She was somewhat…upset. That's why I was worried when I met you. I didn't want to hurt anyone else. But you don't want to get married again, either, so everything's okay. Look, I still have to shave,' he added, rubbing his stubbly chin. 'You could pop in the shower while I'm doing that, if you like.'

'Oh, no, no, no,' Leah said, wagging an index finger at him. 'I'm not falling for that little trick. I'll wait till you're finished. I'd like to shower in peace, then get dressed and go home.'

'Wearing what, pray tell? Your panties are history and that little black number is not quite the thing for day wear.'

'Surely you have something in your wardrobe I can put on.'

'Not a thing,' he said blithely.

'Then you'll have to go out and buy me something.'

'You told me I wasn't to buy you anything except flowers and chocolates.'

'Oh, truly! You're being deliberately difficult. I have to go home eventually.'

'You'll just have to stay here till tonight, won't you? And then you can comfortably wear your black dress home in my car. Without panties, of course. But no one will know that.'

'*You* will.'

His grin was wicked. 'Yes, ma'am. I sure will.'

CHAPTER FIFTEEN

'YOU? AND *JASON*?'

Leah could not help smiling at Trish's surprise. Clearly, she'd done a good job last week of not betraying how attractive she'd found their new boss.

'Yes,' she confirmed. 'Me and Jason.'

The two girls were having morning tea together in the canteen, with Leah feeling she had to explain to Trish what was behind her resignation.

'Oh, you lucky thing!' Trish exclaimed. 'I'll bet he's fabulous in bed. No, you don't have to answer that. But I can see by the look on your face that he is. So, is it serious already? Is that why you're resigning?'

'Partly,' Leah said, and told Trish about Jason wanting her to be in his new advertising campaign.

'I wouldn't be able to keep on working here, Trish, especially once it becomes known I'm going out with the boss. You know what it'd be like. All the girls would talk. So would the reps. There'd be gossip and jealousy and accusations of favouritism.'

'Yeah. There was a bit of that going on when I was sleeping with Jim. Speaking of Jim, I think he's going to be asked to leave.'

'It wouldn't surprise me.'

'Bob said Jason was on to him.'

'Goodness, I forgot you went out with Bob on Friday night. How did that go?'

'Pretty good. It's not love at first sight, but he's a really nice man. We're going out again soon.'

'I'm glad, Trish. Jim was a total waste of your time for a girl who wants to get married and have children.'

'You're dead right. And let's face it, most of us girls do.'

'Yes,' Leah said with what was perhaps a too-wistful sigh.

Trish gave her a sharp look. 'Is there something wrong, Leah? You sounded…sad, just then.'

'No, no, I'm just tired.'

'Too much sex,' Trish said with a knowing little laugh.

'Could be.'

'Lucky you. That's how Jim got me in, you know. He's very good at it. Sex, that is. There again, he's certainly had enough practice,' she added tartly. 'Did you know he was having it off with Shelley as well?'

'Er…yes,' Leah admitted. 'I'm sorry, Trish. I didn't want to be the one to tell you.'

Trish sighed. 'Men like that should be castrated. You're lucky, finding someone like Jason.'

'He's not perfect, Trish.'

'How can you say that? He's utterly gorgeous and rich and nice and rich and utterly gorgeous! What's not perfect about him?' she asked with a frown.

'He doesn't want to get married again.'

'Oh. Oh, I see. Oh, that's too bad.'

'Yes.' Speaking the truth out loud had a very depressing effect on Leah.

'Maybe you should take your own advice then, Leah, and not waste your time on some man who isn't going to give you what *you* want.'

'I fully agree with you. But the problem is…I love him. A lot.'

'Maybe he'll change his mind. If anyone could make a man change his mind, it's you.'

Leah smiled. 'That's a lovely thing to say.'

'You're a lovely person.'

Leah knew she had to change the subject. Quickly.

'Do you think Mandy can do my job?'

'She's a bit young. Jason asked me that first thing this morning and I advised him to stay with a temp for a while. It won't do Mandy any harm to wait a bit.'

'Yes, I think that's wise.'

'You're sounding like you won't be staying much longer.'

'No, no, I won't be. Just a day or two.'

'We're going to miss you. *I'm* going to miss you.'

'We can still go out occasionally together.'

Trish's smile was wry. 'Not if you're going to be dating the boss. Being a billionaire's girlfriend sounds like a full-time after-hours job.'

Leah shook her head. 'It might not be a permanent job.'

Trish reached across the table to touch Leah gently on the wrist. 'You've fallen very hard for him, haven't you?'

Leah was to think about that expression for the rest of the day.

Fallen hard.

It sounded like she'd had an accident; that she'd already hurt herself. Which, in a way, she had.

For what good could come of entering a relationship that was doomed from the start? How was she going to survive it?

At four thirty, Leah tidied her desk and left the office. Jason had wanted her to go home to his place, but she'd insisted on returning to her own apartment at Gladesville on week nights. She'd compromised by suggesting she cook him dinner. Then, if he wanted to, he could stay the night.

He wanted to. Naturally.

On the way home, she stopped at the local shopping centre and picked up the ingredients for dinner. Then she dropped into the news agency and bought herself a diary. Not a large one. Something that she could carry with her and write in when the stress of pretending became too much, because that was what her life was going to be most of the time from now on.

Pretending.

But she would not pretend in her diary. There, she

would put down her real thoughts and feelings. She would say how much she loved Jason. She would express her hopes for the future, no matter how futile they were. She would give voice to her dreams. And her secret desires.

Seven o'clock saw her dressed casually in blue cotton slacks and a blue-and-white striped blouse. Her hair was up in a casual ponytail, her makeup and perfume freshened. A bottle of wine was chilling in the fridge and a Japanese chicken curry was simmering in her electric frypan.

She'd written a few lines in her diary earlier, bringing some release to her anxiety.

The doorbell rang right on time. Jason was, it seemed, a punctual man. Either that, or an eager one.

Leah experienced a mixture of excitement and fear as she went to answer the door. Tonight would set the tone for their relationship. Tonight she had to play the role she thought he wanted her to play.

Schooling her face into a coolly sophisticated smile, she opened the door.

'Come in, darling,' she said. 'Dinner's just about ready.'

CHAPTER SIXTEEN

LEAH RODE THE lift up to the penthouse floor of Jason's building, as she'd ridden it many times before. She had her own private keycard these days.

Six months had passed since she'd agreed to become Jason's girlfriend.

That was what Jason always introduced her as. His girlfriend.

Leah supposed it was a lot better than mistress. Though the tabloids did use that word occasionally.

They had become a rather high-profile couple, their photographs splashed across the gossip pages of magazines and newspapers, especially after she achieved fame in her own right as the face of the Sunshine range of products.

Jason's new advertising and marketing campaign had proved very successful. Beville Holdings was going from strength to strength, with new management and a new receptionist. Mandy. Leah was now a highly sought-after photographic model, a job she quite liked, but which she suspected would eventually run its course.

Her relationship with Jason seemed just as happy—on the surface. They did go out in public together a lot more, to restaurants and parties and other social functions that Jason was invited to. And she occasionally helped him entertain in his penthouse.

But Jason wasn't overly keen on the social side of being a billionaire. Often their weekends were quiet, allowing Leah to still visit the hospital on a Saturday, after which she would go home to visit her father, like in the old days. Jason would always join her there and they would stay overnight.

Mrs B. adored him. Her father liked him, too, despite his not offering to become his son-in-law. Jason was a very likable man.

Yes, everything seemed okay.

Lately, however, Leah would catch Jason looking at her sometimes with a slight frown in his eyes. Something was bothering him about her. She dared not ask him what the matter was, because she feared the answer.

Was he growing bored with her perhaps?

She'd tried terribly hard not to cling, sensing he'd hate that. And she never told him she loved him. Never ever. Not even when he was making love to her in that long, gentle way he did sometimes, and which totally overwhelmed her with emotion. The way he looked down at her as he rocked slowly in and out of her, often brought the words to her lips.

But she always bit them back. Always!

When the lift doors opened, Leah just stood there for a moment. She could hear voices coming from the depths of the open-plan apartment. She hadn't expected company tonight. Friday night they usually spent having dinner in the restaurant that occupied part of the floor below Jason's penthouse, followed by a spa bath, then bed.

Jason hadn't mentioned anything about having anyone over tonight when he'd called her around lunchtime. The thought of having to entertain some of Jason's hyped-up business colleagues did not appeal. Leah felt tired. Tired and dispirited. And worried.

With a weary sigh, she hooked her bag over her shoulder and stepped out of the lift.

Jason's stomach had tightened when he heard the purr of the lift.

It would be Leah, of course. Beautiful, intriguing, enigmatic Leah, coming to spend Friday night with him, as usual.

'That will be Leah now,' he said to Bob and Trish.

Trish beamed from where she was perched on the edge of a black leather armchair, sipping a celebratory glass of champagne. 'I haven't seen Leah in ages. Except on the telly, of course. And on those fabulous billboards.'

'Those billboards are really something, aren't they?' Bob remarked. 'Have you told Leah about us yet, Jase?'

Jason smiled at his obviously very happy PA. 'No. I thought we might surprise her.'

Bob had confided to Jason just after lunch at work that he'd popped the question to Trish the previous night, but hadn't as yet bought a ring. The proposal had been of the impulsive kind. So Jason had given him a hefty cash bonus as an engagement present and sent them both off ring shopping. When Bob had rung him around six to thank him, mentioning that they were on their way to a top city restaurant to celebrate, he'd immediately invited them up to the penthouse for a predinner drink of champagne.

His first thought was to ring Leah, but he'd already rung her twice that day. Telephone calls to Leah were often uncomfortable experiences for Jason. Leah wasn't like other women, or any other girlfriend he'd ever had.

Even Karen—who was the most independent of women—had liked him to call her often. They'd talked for hours on the phone before they were married.

Leah, however, always cut him short on the phone, saying there was something she had to do, or somewhere she had to go. The only time he got to really talk to her alone was during their Friday night dinners. Even then, she had the knack of keeping their conversation to what had happened that day, never the past, or—heaven forbid—the future!

He glanced up and there she was, looking absolutely gorgeous in a forest-green woollen dress that hugged her body and gave his never-ending desire for her no peace at all. Her hair was up in that soft, sexy style he adored. A gold necklace—not one he'd ever bought her—adorned her lovely throat, matching earrings dangling from her small earlobes. Her perfume seemed to precede her into the room, a teasing tantalising scent that drove him insane.

'Trish!' she exclaimed, her beautiful but often too-serious face lighting up when she saw who his visitors were. 'And Bob! I'm so glad it's you and not some of Jason's old cronies.'

'I don't have old cronies,' he protested, and handed her a glass of champagne. 'I'm not your father.'

'You certainly aren't,' she said as she took it, dropping her handbag on an empty chair. 'What are we celebrating?'

Trish jumped up from her chair and wriggled her ring finger at Leah. 'This,' she said.

'Oh, my, you're engaged! How wonderful! And what a lovely ring.'

'The boss paid for most of it,' Bob said, and Leah swung round to smile at him. Yet she didn't really look happy.

Jason wished he could read what it was that made her eyes go like that. So dull and sad. Was she thinking of the time when her husband had given her a diamond ring? Damn and blast, would she ever get over that bastard?

'That was very generous of you, darling,' she said.

Jason winced inside. He hated it when she called him darling like that. It was so superficial sounding. So…meaningless.

He wasn't her darling. He would never be her darling.

What a dismaying thought.

Jason could not pin down the moment he realised he'd fallen in love with Leah. Perhaps it was the Friday night last month when she'd been running terribly late and he hadn't been able to get her on her mobile. A vicious storm had swept in from the west, bringing heavy rain and hail, along with lightning and thunder. He'd paced the rain-soaked terraces, staring out at the storm and worrying his guts out that she'd been one of the many people already involved in car accidents that night. He'd been on the verge of ringing all the hospitals when she'd finally arrived.

There *had* been an accident. In the harbour tunnel. She'd been caught right in the middle at the deepest part and her mobile simply wouldn't work.

Jason recalled feeling physically ill with relief, then being overcome with the need to hold her and make love to her. He'd dragged her down on to the nearest rug and ravaged her, right then and there. He hadn't even bothered to use a condom. Afterwards, when Leah said she'd have to get a morning-after pill, he hadn't wanted her to.

But he'd made no objections at the time.

He'd felt frustrated afterwards because he'd used sex to express his love instead of saying it. He *still* used sex to express his love.

But Leah didn't seem to want anything else from him!

Karen had told him that one day he'd fall in love again. He hadn't believed her at the time. But Karen had been a very wise woman. She knew time would heal his grief.

How much time did Leah need, Jason wondered, to heal her grief? How long could he bear loving her and not being loved back? It was becoming increasingly difficult, especially when he saw the way people in love acted together.

Bob and Trish could not stop touching each other, and looking at each other, their eyes full of love, their talk full of plans.

Leah didn't want to talk about the future at all. She just lived for the day. If he didn't know the good work she did at that hospital every week, he might have thought she'd become very selfish.

'We should toast the happy couple,' Jason proposed. 'To Bob and Trish.'

'And to love,' Trish added, clinking her glass against Bob's.

Jason saw Leah's reaction. Instantly negative.

It was another defining moment in Jason's life, the moment he decided that he could not go on with this relationship. Not the way it was.

Something had to give. He hoped that something would be Leah.

He's going to break up with me, Leah realised when their eyes met.

Her heart recoiled. So did her stomach.

'I'm sorry, everyone,' she said, and swiftly put her glass down. 'But I...I have to go to the bathroom.'

Leah fairly raced for the guest powder room, only just reaching it before her stomach heaved. It wasn't the first time that day. Or that week.

A pregnancy test this afternoon had confirmed her fear.

She was going to have Jason's baby.

Leah knew exactly when it had happened. The night of the storm. She should have gone to the doctor the very next morning. But she hadn't. She just couldn't.

And now here she was, having Jason's child. And he didn't want her any more.

'Are you all right, Leah?' Jason asked from the other idea of the door.

Leah leant a clammy cheek against the cubicle wall. 'Yes, I...er...must have eaten something that didn't agree with me. Sorry. I'll be out in a minute.'

'Bob and Trish have a booking for seven.'

'Tell them to go. Please. I might be longer here than a minute.'

'Will do.'

Leah stayed in the powder room for five more minutes, not emerging till she knew the coast was clear. The apartment was deathly quiet as she returned to the living room. Jason was standing at one of the largest of the plate-glass windows, his hands in his trousers pockets, his back to her. He could have been just standing there, watching the city lights, but Leah knew he wasn't. He was trying to find the right words to say to her.

Leah decided to help him out.

'It's all right, Jason,' she said tautly. 'You can just say it. I won't make a scene.'

He turned slowly, his handsome face more bleak than she'd even seen it. 'Say what, exactly?'

'That we're finished.'

'Is that what you want me to say, Leah?'

She could not stop the shudder from running down her spine. 'No!'

His expression startled her, because it carried surprise. 'You don't?'

Leah found her insides dissolving, along with the façade she'd carried all these months. 'Why on earth would I want you to say that?' she threw at him. 'I *love* you, Jason. I've loved you all this time.'

Jason could not believe how angry her declaration made him.

'*Love* me?' he threw back at her. 'You don't honestly expect me to believe that, do you? I know what it feels like when a woman loves me, and it isn't what I feel when I'm with you, madam. You don't really talk to me, even when we're together. All you want from me is what we share in bed.'

'That's because that's all you offered me!' she countered, startling him with *her* anger. 'If you think I've enjoyed this past six months with you, Jason, then you can think again. It's been hell, I tell you, pretending not to love you. If you don't believe me, then I've got something I think you should read.'

Read? 'What?'

'This.'

He watched in total confusion whilst she walked over and pulled a small black book from her handbag. He almost dropped it when she tossed it at him from a distance.

He stared at the cover. 'It's a diary.'

'Yes. *Mine.* I wrote in it whenever the pretence became too much for me.'

'But why in heaven's name would you think you had to pretend?' he asked.

She shook her head in a highly agitated fashion. 'And I thought you were an intelligent man. Because you told me right at the beginning that you couldn't possibly love me back, that's why!'

'Yes, I did, didn't I?' he murmured, his heart catching as he read the first entry. It was dated back in February.

I must remember never to tell Jason that I love him. He'll break up with me if I do. But I can tell you. I love him. I love him. I love him. Now I must go. He'll be here shortly for dinner. I can't wait.

Those last three words touched Jason the most. He flicked on through the pages, searching for last month's entries, knowing that she was sure to have written something about that night as well.

Yes! There it was.

Dreadfully late getting to Jason's place tonight. Traffic accident in the tunnel. At first I thought he was genuinely worried about me. That maybe he loved me. But that wasn't it. He just wanted sex, as usual. On the floor, no less. Without using protection. I wanted to cry afterwards. I almost did when he agreed with my suggestion that I go to the doctor for the morning-after pill. I don't want to go, but I guess I will. Dear God, it's cruel to love someone like this...

He looked up, his heart filled to overflowing with regret, and sadness. If only he'd known...

Slowly, however, the realisation of Leah's love sank in, and an unbelievable joy blossomed in Jason's chest.

'She really loves me, Karen,' he whispered.

Yes, my dearest, he thought he heard her reply.

Undoubtedly, it was only his imagination speaking to him.

But that didn't matter, because Jason knew Karen would be genuinely happy for him. A generous woman, Karen. A lovely, brave, generous woman.

'*What* did you say?' Leah asked, her eyes widening.

Jason walked slowly towards her. 'I said I love you, too.'

She blinked. 'You *do*?'

'I do,' he repeated.

'Then why on earth didn't you *say* so?'

'For the same reasons you didn't,' he explained, cupping her face and looking deep into her frustrated green eyes. 'I thought you didn't *want* me to love you. I thought you still loved your first husband.'

'But I don't. And I didn't say that I did. I just said people usually marry for love. But you, Jason, you definitely said you were still in love with your wife.'

'I do still love her. But that hasn't stopped me falling in love with you, Leah. Karen told me before she died that I would find someone else, someone special, someone more my age who would love me and give me children. Karen couldn't have children, you see. She'd had cancer of the cervix when she was younger.'

'Oh. But that's so sad. I didn't realise she'd had cancer before. The poor woman.'

'She was an amazing woman. And I did love her. But you are even more amazing, Leah, and I love you madly. Will you marry me and have my children?'

'Well…yes, of course I will. But…'

'But what?'

'Oh, dear. I hope you're not going to be cross with me.'

'Out with it, girl.'

'That night of the storm,' she blurted out.

'Yes, I just read that bit.'

'I…er…I didn't go to the doctor the next day.'

'And?'

'I took a pregnancy test today, and it was positive.'

Once Jason got his head around the fact that he was already a father, he could not contain his delight.

'Leah, that's fantastic!' he cried, hugging her to him. 'I couldn't be happier. A baby. Already.' He pulled back to hold her by the shoulders. 'We'll get married as soon as possible. And we'll go house hunting. I know how much you hate this place.'

'It's not so bad,' she said. 'I've gotten used to it. But not quite the place to raise children. You don't just want one baby, do you, Jason? I want at least two.'

'Have as many as you like.'

Tears filled Leah's eyes. 'I can't believe everything has turned out all right,' she said, still half-fearful of such happiness. 'I thought tonight was going to be the end.'

'Never. I was going to make you marry me, whether you loved me or not.'

Leah blinked back her tears. 'Really? *How?*'

'I have no idea. Bribery and corruption. No, probably persuasion and negotiation. That's what I'm best at. I would have worked out what you wanted more than me and given it to you in exchange for a ring on your finger. Which reminds me. First thing tomorrow we're going ring shopping. And I'm going to buy the biggest, flashiest, most expensive diamond ring in Sydney.'

Leah laughed. 'Has it been very hard on you, my telling you not to buy me anything over a hundred dollars?'

'Extremely. Now that I've been let off the hook, I'm going to go crazy, buying you things.'

'There is something which you could buy me. Two things, actually…'

'I'll get them for you tomorrow. Tell me.'

Leah smiled. Buying her mother's house would not be achieved in a day. But Leah was sure her father would sell it to them, along with the boat in the boathouse.

How wonderful it would be to raise her family there with Jason by her side as her husband. A real husband this time. A man she could depend on. A man who loved her as much as she loved him.

'It's going to cost you a lot of money,' she said teasingly, knowing her father would drive a hard bargain.

'Leah, I am a seriously rich man. There's nothing I can't buy.'

Except love, Jason realised. That was never for sale. Not true love.

'You're going to have to deal with a ruthless negotiator,' she warned him.

'I can be pretty ruthless myself. Look, just tell me who you're talking about and what it is you want.'

When Leah told him, Jason tried not to smile. Joachim had already expressed the wish on a recent visit to the penthouse that he'd love to live in a place just like it. Clearly, his future father-in-law was ready for a change.

'Piece of cake, my darling,' he said, his face breaking into a broad smile. 'Piece of cake.'

CHAPTER SEVENTEEN

JOACHIM KNELT DOWN to put the champagne-coloured roses in the vase built into Isabel's marble gravestone. She'd loved that colour of rose, ever since she'd had them in her wedding bouquet.

'Well, my darling,' he murmured. 'I did what you wanted and you were right. He was the man for our Leah.'

Joachim fell silent for a few moments, thinking of all the times during their marriage that Isabel had cleverly got her point across, softly, subtly, without nagging. People often thought he wore the pants in their family. He would once have thought so, too.

But he wasn't so sure now. It wasn't till after Isabel had died that he realised how much he'd relied on her advice. And her very wise ways. She was an extremely intuitive woman. Especially about people.

Of course, being a very egotistical man, Joachim hadn't always agreed with Isabel.

'You never did like Carl, did you?' he went on softly.

'You said as much the day Leah married him, but I didn't listen to you. I listened to you this time, didn't I? They were married yesterday, at home. Their home, now. A quiet ceremony with Mrs B. doing the catering. She's staying on with them, by the way. Oh, and I bought Jason's penthouse. I needed to finally move on, Isabel. I hope you understand.'

Joachim smiled. 'I dare say you already know about the baby. And that it's going to be a boy. He and I are going to be great mates. We'll go sailing together, and camping, and fishing. Yes, Isabel, I happen to like camping and fishing. You don't know everything about me. I'll bet you never imagined I'd be talking to you like this. You always called me an old sceptic about God and heaven and the afterlife.'

Joachim stood up, stroking the grass from his trousers. 'Of course, I know you're probably not still actually *here*, my darling. But you're somewhere nearby, aren't you, still looking over me and Leah.'

Tears pricked at Joachim's eyes. Enough, he told himself, and blinked them away. Life went on.

'I must go, Isabel. I have lots to do. I have to buy a four-wheel drive, for one thing. And lots of fishing and camping gear. Yes, you're right again. I have no idea how to do either, but I can learn.'

As Joachim swung away, his attention was caught by the name on the headstone next to Isabel's.

POLLACK.

He hadn't noticed it before. He frowned as he stared down at the simple inscription.

'Karen Pollack,' he read aloud. 'Beloved wife of Jason Pollack. A lovely, brave, generous woman.'

Joachim stared at it for a very long time, then he smiled and walked slowly away.

0406/05a

MILLS & BOON®

Live the emotion

In May 2006, By Request presents two collections of three favourite romances by our bestselling Mills & Boon authors:

Australian Playboy Tycoons

by Miranda Lee

The Playboy's Proposition
The Playboy's Virgin
The Playboy in Pursuit

Make sure you buy these irresistible stories!

On sale 5th May 2006

Available at WHSmith, Tesco, ASDA, Borders, Eason, Sainsbury's and most bookshops

www.millsandboon.co.uk